Claire,
After All

Karen J. Hasley

This is a work of fiction. The characters described herein are imaginary and are not intended to refer to living persons.

Claire, After All
All Rights Reserved
Copyright@2014

This book may not be reproduced, transmitted, or stored in whole or in part by any means without the express written consent of the author except in brief quotations contained in critical articles and/or reviews.

ISBN-13: 978-1500665265
ISBN-10: 1500665266

1837

Chapter 1

*L*ooking at her family, Lady Claire Penwarren experienced a wave of pride and affection so powerful that for one brief moment she teetered on the edge of tears, a display of emotion that would have been both rare and out of character. Fortunately for all concerned, the improbable tears never materialized, but Claire still felt a deep and lingering sentiment. The objects of her attention were such good traveling companions—no whining or moping and between her brothers only a few boyish scuffles that were harmless enough and perfectly understandable—that she did not consider her strong feelings to be self-indulgent or unfairly partial.

The trip from India had been long and demanding, twelve weeks on the ocean and now a third day on land en route to West Sussex from their docking at Bristol. Yet there had not been one complaining peep out of any of them. She knew her sister Cecelia must be fatigued, cold from the late winter wind, and apprehensive, but from all appearances she was serene and agreeable, smiling in her usual congenial way. Claire was appreciatively aware that her sister would maintain her equanimity at any cost so as not to cause worry or distress. Cece's generous nature was as precious as her beauty.

The boys, God bless them, still hadn't tired of the adventure. Of course, they were eleven so everything would remain an adventure to them for at least another year or two, but they were affectionate and amusing, careful not to cause either of their sisters any concern. Really, Claire thought with rush of gratitude, I have the best family in the world, and she followed up with a quick, silent thank-you to her father for always setting her up to her siblings as the one with authority.

She could still see him in the great, airy hallway of their sparkling Indian home hugging them one by one and saying in his sternly affable way, "Now Claire's in charge and I don't want to hear that you've given her a moment's grief. She'll make good decisions, and you're to trust her as much as I do and do what she says." Then he'd grabbed both boys into another huge hug, given Cecelia a gentler embrace, and come to stand before Claire taking both her hands in his. "My dear, I have every confidence in you. All the arrangements are made, with a coach waiting in Bristol and word sent to your Aunt Sophie to expect you. I've forwarded funds for your use with instructions to old Billcote to give you whatever you ask. You have his address, and I know you won't hesitate to approach him. I have no doubt you'll have your usual excellent success. You've never given me one cause for concern, Claire, and with you making the decisions I've never had to worry about anything. I'm the one who'll rattle around this big house like a pebble in a bottle. I don't want to think about what it will be like with all of you gone," and he'd blinked back sudden tears as he bent and kissed her on the cheek.

Claire's heart had given a little twist at her father's words, but she refused to trouble him with tears of her own, only smiled and said in return, "I'll take good care of them, Papa. I promise. Don't worry about a thing, and we'll expect that you'll join us within the year."

She'd turned to wave out the carriage window as they pulled away from the house and thought he looked bereft and alone, despite the air of easy confidence he always wore. Claire knew her father well, understood his moods and his expectations and had acted as his hostess practically since childhood—kept his house, directed the servants, entertained visitors, and raised his children. She was his rock, he her hero, and despite the presence of her sister and brothers for a moment Claire had felt as lost and abandoned as her father looked, staring after the departing coach with his hands jammed into his pockets. Then Cece caught her eye and smiled her understanding, and Claire's calm and practical good nature resurfaced. Her papa had entrusted his dearest possessions into her hands, and she would see them safely to England and their new home that lay halfway around the world. She had never failed at anything he'd asked of her, and there was no reason this undertaking should be any different.

The voyage was unexceptional, calm for the most part and warm much of the way. The boys made quick friends with the sailors and spent the better part of each day asking endless questions and getting underfoot. Despite that—or perhaps because of it—they quickly became the pets of captain and crew. Cece had spent her days in needlework and reading, never tiring of either to Claire's amazement. Claire herself chafed at sedentary occupations and was up early every morning for several brisk walks around the deck. She admitted to herself that she was envious of her brother's freedom. The boys were allowed to disport themselves with relative abandon, climbing ropes and racing like wild creatures from stem to stern. Her liberties must be more restrained.

As they rounded the Horn and sailed north, the weather slowly changed. Cold winds forced Cece from the deck entirely and into her cabin and compelled Claire to bundle up in layers before she headed out for her morning walk. By the time they reached Bristol, Claire and her brothers had somewhat adjusted to the difference in climate. Not so Cece, who began to shiver upon entering English waters and could not seem to stop, although she felt ashamed of her reaction and never complained of the cold.

Once in port, Betcher was waiting for them with a handsome gentleman's coach pulled by four magnificent and perfectly matched bays. Claire had been told to expect both Betcher and the coach and as usual her father's directions were accurate to the most refined detail. Over the protests of her brothers, who each proclaimed that if he didn't see the famous *Jessop's Floating Harbor* his life would be incomplete and devoid of any hope of future joy, she told Betcher to load up their baggage and depart immediately for home. Claire hoped no one noticed how unnatural, how clumsy even, the word *home* sounded from her lips. She would never have admitted it aloud, but she doubted she would ever consider the Loden Valley of West Sussex to be home. Her dreams overflowed with the vivid colors of the place she considered her true home: Assam in Northern India, a lush corner of the world, luxuriantly warm and green and nothing like the dull brown countryside she saw outside the carriage window with patches of snow still dotting the landscape. They might as well have landed on a distant star. If she felt this way, it must be even worse for her sister.

Claire rested a hand on Cece's arm and asked, "All right?"

Cecelia, who had been gazing down at her gloved hands, raised her brown eyes with their luxuriant black lashes and lifted one hand to lace her fingers with Claire's.

"Yes, but these last days traveling on land seem to pass more slowly than the whole ocean voyage. Are we almost home?"

Claire recognized the same uncertainty in the concluding word that she had tried to keep from her own tone earlier.

"I think so. Just a few more hours now, Betcher said, and then I'm sure Aunt Sophie will have warm fires burning and a hearty meal on the table for us. We have only one more stop."

Matthew, overhearing from his place in the corner, gave a whoop. "Then I can trade with Will and ride up top, can't I? You said we'd trade each time we stopped."

"I can't imagine why you think riding out in the elements is attractive, Matthew, but a deal is a deal and when we stop next Will can come in with us and you can ride with Betcher. If that's what you want."

"It is what I want! Betcher says the only man with better hands than him is someone named Symonton. You should see Betcher handle the reins. I'd be happy if I could do half that well. Do you think I'll have the chance to learn once we get to Loden Hall?" Claire met her brother's eager look with a smiling one of her own.

"Papa said Uncle Thomas always kept quality stables and livestock so I wouldn't be surprised, but we'll have to wait and ask Aunt Sophie's permission first."

"Why do we have to ask her leave?" Matthew rejoined with unconscious arrogance. "She's not in charge any more."

Claire liked neither the tone nor the content of that remark and replied coolly, "We will always have to be respectful to our elders, and especially now to Aunt Sophie." Then to soften her words somewhat she added, "You'll have plenty of time to learn everything you're interested in, Matt, and you won't regret being kind in the bargain."

It was clear from his expression that he already wished he hadn't said what he did and because his older sister's good opinion was as dear to him as gold, he just nodded and settled back into the corner of the seat to stare out the window. Claire was the only mother the boy had ever known and while at eleven it wasn't something he would or even could express, he loved her and wouldn't have purposefully displeased her for anything.

At the last coach stop everyone got out to stretch as Betcher refreshed the team. Claire lifted out a small wooden carrier from where it had rested next to her feet and handed it to her brothers.

"Put Babu on his leash and let him roam a little; he's been complaining the last few miles. I'll see if I can find some cream for him."

She linked arms with Cece and the two went inside the coach house to find seats by the fire. A young man was already seated there, and Claire didn't miss the glance he gave her sister. He looked to be presentable, well-groomed and respectably dressed, and it was only the one glance, after all, but the attention, however subtle, still caused a small frown to appear between Claire's brows. More often than not, men looked at Cecelia exactly as the young man had—a first casual scan and then a sudden and more intent second look that could be almost comical, as if they couldn't believe what they'd seen. Cece, as usual oblivious to the reaction her appearance caused in the opposite sex, pulled a stool closer to the flames and sat down, holding both palms out toward the fire.

"Babu needs milk," Claire explained to her sister. "They must have a little to spare here and perhaps a little meat, too. Will you be all right if I leave you alone for a few minutes?"

Cecelia, with a good-humored twist to her mouth, answered, "You worry too much about me, Claire. I'm not a little girl any more and I'll be fine. I'd come with you, but I want to soak up as much of this warmth as I can before we set off again."

It was precisely because Cecelia wasn't a little girl that Claire worried. She sent one more sidelong look in the direction of the young man who sat with his hands around a mug of something—hopefully nothing stronger than tea—at one of the tables across the room, decided he was a minimal risk, and went in search of the kitchens.

"Hello," Claire called, stepping into a hallway.

A woman came out of a large side room, wiping her hands on her apron. "Yes, ma'am?"

"I wondered if there was a little cream and some fish we could have. I'll pay you for them, of course."

"Cream and fish?" the woman repeated in a tone that said the combination was both baffling and repellent. Her opinion was reflected in her expression, as well.

"Oh, not for me," explained Claire, laughing. "It does sound awful, doesn't it? It's for our cat. He's been locked up all day and has begun to complain about being hungry. When Babu complains, we are all forced to listen. He has a wail that's caused him to be banned in several cities."

The woman, like so many other people before her, was no match for Claire's friendly smile and frank manners. She could tell that Claire was quality by her speech and dress but there was something else besides, something not as easily defined, a certain transparent honesty or integrity of character that showed itself in Claire's face. To the cook, the woman standing before her was what all women of quality should be but seldom were. Nose not too high but not overly familiar, either. This young woman had got it exactly right.

The cook's morning had been one nuisance after another. The hens had somehow escaped their pen and had to be shooed back in. She'd blistered her hand taking a hot pan of bread from the oven and subsequently dropped both pan and bread onto the floor, and that in turn had brought sharp, hurtful words from her husband. But at that moment if Claire had asked for the moon, the cook would cheerfully have gone in search of a ladder.

"I can find some cream but there's naught of fish in the kitchen. Would a little mutton do?"

"Even better. A little variety in his diet will put him in good temper, and we will all thank you for that."

When the cook returned with the feline treats, Claire expressed her gratitude, silently slipped the woman a coin, and went outside in search of her brothers, who had tied Babu's leash to a railing pole and were listening enrapt to Betcher's racing tales. Claire stopped for just a minute to study the scene.

The boys would seem identical to strangers, but to her they were so dearly individual and unique they might not have been twins at all. Matthew, the elder by five minutes, was intensely protective of anything weak or vulnerable, quick-tempered and as quickly contrite, not easily given to studies but athletic and strong and active. William, barely taller than his brother and with hair a shade lighter, was of a more imaginative, thoughtful temperament. Fortunately, since the five minutes made all the difference to inheritance, Will was very bright and possessed an extraordinarily sensitive conscience that did not allow him to question or complain. He knew he would not succeed his father as the next Earl of Loden, knew what that meant to his future prospects, and truly did not care. He was more interested in the sciences and in why mechanical things worked the way they did, interested in nature and living creatures for the same reason. Being an earl would be a bother, Will once stated seriously, and would get in the way of the future he had planned for himself, scientist or explorer or both. There wasn't an ounce of jealousy or mean spirit in him.

Both brothers were fiercely loyal to each other, so close they could finish each other's sentences—probably their thoughts, too—if they chose. Claire had loved them as her own from the first moment she'd seen them as newborns sleeping side-by-side in a woven basket, their arms across each other even then. Now, watching them with their chins resting on their fists, identical profiles listening enthralled to Betcher's stories of equestrian adventures, she could only smile. They were as much a part of her mission as was Cecelia, and she would not disappoint her father or the boys.

Babu, a lean, white cat, rose at Claire's approach, meowed a throaty, strangely musical greeting, and when Claire paused to observe her brothers, began to try to twist out of his collar and leash. With his usual sense of entitlement, Babu had decided that if Claire would not rush to him with supper, he must get to her to remind her of her duties. He had tried similar escapes before without success, but because hope sprang ever eternal in his feline breast, he threw himself onto his side, contorted his neck so that he formed an almost perfect circle, and slowly pulled his head back. Such twists and turns had never worked previously, but—wonder of wonders!—this time they did. The collar slowly slipped over the cat's ears and then off his head entirely, and he was no longer restrained. For just a moment Babu could not quite believe his good fortune and sniffed the collar lying on the ground as if it were some strange creature that had suddenly dropped from the heavens. Then putting it all together in his remarkably agile brain, the cat gave a quick spring away. His original goal had been to reach Claire, enveloped as she was in the seductive smell of mutton, but the sudden sense of invigorating freedom distracted him. He realized that he could go anywhere he pleased, no carrier, no collar, no demeaning leash—a *canine* contrivance hardly appropriate for an animal once rightfully worshipped as divine—so when out of the corner of one eye he spied a small streak of gray dart across the yard, Babu did not think twice. Having been locked up for more weeks than any self-respecting cat should be forced to be confined, he was not about to miss his chance to prove that he had retained all his fierce rodent-hunting skills. Ignoring the horses and carriage drawing near the posting house and with the mouse in his sights, Babu gave a piercing yowl that might have come from something much larger and fiercer and crossed the lane at breakneck speed, a streak of snarling white that startled the approaching horses and caused them to veer to the side and rear up snorting. Only the steady, skilled hands of the driver kept the contrivance upright and out of the ditch.

Claire, still contemplating her brothers, missed the cat's initial escape and turned just in time to see the white streak that was Babu cross the lane in pursuit of something she couldn't see but which Babu must have found irresistible. She called his name, dropped the food from her hands, and ran after the cat. Matthew, first to realize what had happened, began to give chase, too, and Will, ever the thinker, stopped to scoop up the fallen mutton before he followed them toward the small copse of bushes into which Babu had darted.

After a moment of thrashing around in the brush, Claire stood upright, knocking her bonnet askew on a low limb as she did so, and said to her brothers, "He'll never come with all of us making this noise. I'm going back to Cece. Matt, stop rummaging around like a bull elephant and stand still. Will, hold out the mutton so Babu gets a whiff of it. He's hungry enough that he will find you instead of the other way around. I'll tell Betcher we can't leave until we find the vexing creature."

Claire stepped up the little incline intent on setting her hat straight and nearly ran into someone standing in her path.

"I beg your pardon," she said, her forehead nearly colliding with the person's chin, and looked up. A man stood before her, and from the look on his face she could tell he was decidedly out of temper. He was hatless but wore a heavy riding greatcoat and fine leather gloves. The driver of the carriage, she supposed, and not happy about the interruption.

Claire retreated a step, put on her most charming smile, and said, "I do truly beg your pardon, sir. I hope we didn't do you or your livestock any harm."

From his tone it was evident that the man had no intention of being charmed. "Madam, did it ever occur to you that the season is somewhat bitter for parades? That white streaking creature was bad enough, but to be followed by two shouting boys and a shrieking woman—your hat remains crooked, by the way—was enough to disrupt even the best of animals. The ground remains slick, as well, so you or those two miscreants stomping around in the bushes could have been injured if I hadn't managed to pull up in time."

Claire had never been cowed by a man, bad-tempered or otherwise, in her life, so as she rearranged her bonnet yet again she said in a soothing voice, "I don't recall shrieking, but except for that minor detail, you are absolutely right, and I don't blame you one bit for being annoyed. I'm sure I'd feel exactly the same were I in your shoes, but to be sensible, no damage occurred to anyone or anything and I believe it is unhealthy to mope too long over things that could have happened but did not."

"I am not moping," the man interjected crossly as Claire continued with blithe good humor.

"We've become inordinately fond of Babu, and while I can understand that might seem both incomprehensible and irrelevant to you because Babu will never pull a carriage or win a race, we can't help ourselves. And to his defense, like the rest of us he's been cooped up for weeks and can hardly be blamed for taking some exercise. I'm only sorry that his constitutional took him directly across your path."

From behind them Matt cried, "Gotcha!" with a satisfied tone and the two boys reappeared next to their sister, Matt holding the white cat tightly in his arms. Babu, content that he'd given that despicable rodent the scare of its life, allowed the embrace. A little piece of mutton clung indecorously to one whisker. Claire fixed a stern look at the offending feline.

"What a nuisance you are!" she said but diluted the scold by reaching a hand to rub the cat's forehead with familiar affection. "If all the cream hasn't drained away, why don't you boys take Babu back to his carrier and put his meal in with him? Then carry him in next to Cece and they can keep warm by the fire together."

Matt, his hands full of cat but his eyes on the two horses being soothed by a stable hand in the small courtyard, said admiringly, "I say, sir, that's a capital team!"

"Indeed," replied the man, still refusing to be cajoled by either common sense or flattery.

"I believe we all owe this gentleman an apology," Claire stated to her brothers, "since we let our affection for Babu interrupt his journey, although I daresay—" Claire's calm voice took on an aspect of quiet introspection "—this was his destination, after all, and he would have slowed down regardless of Babu's involvement. Still—"

She eyed her brothers in an expectant manner and they responded, "We're awfully sorry, sir," the words spoken in chorus and both faces suitably contrite.

The apology had the desired effect. Claire saw a momentary appreciative gleam of amusement in the man's eyes. Her brothers' ability to speak in tandem and look sheepishly penitent, two sides of the same mirror, had gotten them out of innumerable scrapes. Even their father was not immune to the effect. The only person the boys knew who could remain unmoved by the contrived display was Claire herself.

Claire, detecting an infinitesimal thaw in the man's original icy hauteur, gave Matt a gentle shove and sent both boys away before they lost the ground they'd taken, then ventured another look at the gentleman. His eyes, originally the color of aquamarine, had warmed to a chilly blue.

She thought that might be the best she could expect and said, "Truly, sir, we are very sorry, and I am sincerely relieved that neither you nor your animals—nor my brothers for that matter—were injured. Babu," she added thoughtfully, "is another story all together. I believe a little knock would have done him good. Cats are so superior, don't you think?"

She caught another gleam of humor before he answered, "I confess that my background with cats is limited."

"Really? Then you've missed an enlightening education in self-centeredness and vanity."

"Not at all. I have several female friends." Claire looked at him quickly and smiled at his innocent expression.

"I'm sure I deserved that for inconveniencing you, and I promise you I feel properly rebuked." Over the man's shoulder, Claire saw the boys come out of the posting house and head for the man's horses. "Oh, dear, I need to catch my brothers before they cause you an additional nuisance. They're enamored of horses and will pester you with questions and attention if I don't stop them."

Following closely behind the twins was the young man that had earlier been sitting inside. Claire saw his gaze move from her to her companion, who had wordlessly fallen into step beside her as she moved toward the courtyard to intercept the twins.

"Symonton!" the younger man called and walked quickly toward them. "I thought it must be you from the boys' description. How do you do, sir?" There was genuine affection in his voice as he reached out a hand.

"Fine, no thanks to this young woman and those two rapscallion boys," but the anger was gone from the man's tone, replaced by a touch of laughter and welcome. He took the extended hand and gave it a firm shake. "Have you been waiting long, Harry?"

"No, hardly at all, and I had good company."

Claire's ears picked up at that. She'd left him alone with Cecelia for longer than was safe for either Cece or the young man and his comment must certainly refer to her sister.

He turned from his uncle to Claire and continued, "Allow me to introduce myself. I'm Harry Macapee, and I chatted briefly with your sister about your trip. You've all had a long go of it."

He was so pleasant and handsome Claire couldn't be offended, but she thought it had not been quite the thing for him to strike up a conversation with an unattended, gently-bred woman in front of a posting inn's fire. She knew Cece would never have initiated the dialogue.

"Yes, we have, but we're close to our destination now, and I've assured all of us, including the cat, that there will be warm fires and a groaning table waiting for us when we arrive."

The young man, some veiled emotion in his eyes Claire could not decipher, remarked without noticeable inflection, "They're on their way to Loden Hall, Uncle." The driver of the carriage turned to look at Claire unblinkingly from those chilly eyes.

"Indeed, madam? Then I believe we will be part-time neighbors. I'm Symonton."

The name meant nothing to Claire, who dipped a perfunctory curtsy and extended her hand, but she was curious about the message the two men had just wordlessly exchanged. Something about Loden Hall, she thought, and stored it away for future consideration.

"How do you do? I'm Claire Penwarren."

Symonton touched her hand briefly with his fingertips. "Philip's daughter?"

"One of them, yes."

Symonton examined her with an absorbed, almost improper interest that gave her leave to do the same. The man had a disquieting look about him with those light blue eyes, dark brows, and white-gold hair, which from a distance had made him seem older than he really was. His lean, brown face with its saturnine twist belonged to a man in his prime despite the hair.

Claire turned to the younger man. "You met my sister Cecelia, then?"

A familiar look was on Macapee's face, the look of a man who had experienced a vision, a man smitten and awed by an undeserved glimpse of Paradise.

"Oh, yes. Yes, indeed. I meant nothing unseemly. We were sharing the fire and conversation just sprang up."

Symonton, watching Claire, saw a smile so fleeting it might never have been before she responded, "I'm sure it did. Cece sometimes has a disarming effect on even the best of intentions."

Will appeared at Claire's elbow to stand respectfully and reproachfully silent until his sister's sidelong glance gave him permission to speak.

"Betcher says we have to go if we want to get to the Hall before dark." The boy turned to Symonton. "He says, sir, that you have the best hands in the county."

"Only in the county?" Claire murmured and took her brother's arm. "I'd have imagined his fame to go much farther than West Sussex. The moon perhaps?" Symonton glanced at her sharply, caught the teasing look in her eyes, and for just a moment found himself in easy humor with her. It had been a long time since he had felt anything so uncomplicated about any woman. She repeated her apology to him, offered a polite farewell to both men, and went inside with her brother.

"What do you think their reaction will be when they reach the Hall?" the younger man asked his uncle.

"I wouldn't hazard a guess, Harry, but if anyone can handle the situation at Loden Hall, she will be the one. You met the sister?" Symonton saw the same look on his nephew's face that Claire had recognized. "Apparently you did, and she must be a diamond to put that besotted look on your face."

Harry shook his head a little ruefully but remained in awe. "Diamond wouldn't be right to describe her. More like ruby or emerald, something rich and exotic. You're bound to meet her, and you'll see. I doubt if our little corner of the world has ever seen anything like her." His uncle turned on his heel.

"This promises to be a month of entertainments. I may stay longer than I had first intended if your mother will have me." Harry followed him to the curricle.

"You know Mother would be pleased if you took up residence with us permanently." He climbed up next to his uncle on the seat. "Too bad you find us all so boring."

From his high seat Symonton watched as Claire, accompanied by a bundled Cecelia holding the cat carrier and the two boys, herded her little group toward their waiting coach. There was a great deal of chattering and laughing, and once Claire had to stop and handle a small argument between the brothers before she, her sister, and one of the twins were handed inside. The remaining boy scrambled up top with the agility of a monkey.

"This is the best!" he shouted down to the others and Symonton heard Claire's response.

"Try to be gracious in victory, Matt. It's much more becoming in the long run," but there was affection and laughter in her voice.

Out of nowhere Symonton recalled his mother using that same warmly indulgent tone when dealing with him and his sister. With his father, too, but that had been more difficult for her and less successful. He gave a frown. Where had that reminiscence come from? He hadn't thought of his own childhood in many years and had few clear memories of his mother when he did. She had died too young.

The coach carrying the Penwarrens pulled out of the drive with Matt waving energetically from his perch as he passed the two men. The boy looked as if someone had given him a great present, hanging on and grinning despite the bumps and sway. He was obviously thrilled with the experience. Symonton gave himself a mental shake. He couldn't remember the last time he'd experienced honest delight and for a moment felt almost wistful about it. It must be the decrepitude of age or just the long, bleak, boring winter he'd had to endure that was responsible for this sudden, small, unsettling flash of nostalgia. He did not appreciate the sensation.

"Uncle?" Curiosity and trepidation warred in young Macapee's voice.

Symonton, seated and fitting on his gloves with precise, deliberate pulls, spoke quietly. "Hang on, Harry," was all he said, but it was enough to cause Harry to take a deep breath and tighten his grip.

The two men pulled off with a smooth rush, overtook the Penwarrens' coach, and passed it so closely that Harry saw a woman's white face peering out the window.

Once out ahead, Harry exhaled audibly, relaxed his hold, and asked, "Do you feel better now, Uncle?"

"Yes," answered Symonton, but in truth he felt a little ashamed of himself for showing off. He hadn't known the need to impress anyone for ages and suddenly recognizing the urge in himself was unexpected, unwelcome, and unpleasant. Inexplicably he felt he'd been bested by a tall, slim, hazel-eyed woman past her first youth, and he didn't know why that should bother him—or intrigue him, whatever it was he felt.

He wished he could be there when she first stepped inside Loden Hall because if anything could discomfit her, it would be that first inspection of her new home. She seemed so self-possessed that he would have liked to have seen her face at that particular moment just to discover if there was anything able to unsettle that relentlessly cheerful equilibrium.

Chapter 2

*D*espite her intentions, Claire spent little time wondering about the silent message that had passed between Symonton and his nephew. Curiosity had been replaced by concern. Cecelia, in her own quiet way, did nothing but comment about the younger man the entire remainder of the trip: his pleasant manners, his amusing anecdotes, his respectful bearing. Alarm bells began clanging inside Claire's head from the start of the conversation.

"We don't know anything about him," she told Cecelia bluntly, but Cece only gave a small, satisfied, rather unsettling smile in return.

"He will be our neighbor." The peal of Claire's alarm bells increased as Cecelia continued, "His mother is a widow. He has an older married sister and an older brother that inherited the title and the property. I think he said his father was the Earl of Pasturson, but titles still confuse me. Harry said—"

"Harry already?" asked Claire, raising both brows at her sister, who had the grace to blush in response.

"Mr. Macapee, I mean. Mr. Macapee said he will be going into the military, that his uncle is buying him a commission."

That settled it, thought Claire, a younger son who would be following the drum was hardly the match she envisioned for her sister, but she had learned quite a bit raising three motherless children and said only, "How generous of his uncle!"

"Yes, isn't it? But Harry—I mean Mr. Macapee—made it a point to tell me that his uncle was a Marquis with no children of his own and that he had volunteered to do so. Mr. Macapee told me he would never have asked for so generous an offer. I think he must be a principled man." Claire, who had her doubts about being able to uncover any man's principles in one forty-minute talk in front of a fire only nodded.

"We can hope so, though if it weren't for Papa, I would wonder if such a being really existed." William and Cecelia shared a surprised look. It was unusual for their cheerful older sister to sound so cynical, and they supposed that the long journey had taken a toll on her spirits. It was so infrequent a happening, Claire being the one who could be counted on to cheer and encourage the rest of the family no matter what difficult situation loomed, that the two younger siblings spent the remainder of the trip trying to amuse her. Claire enjoyed their attention and used the time to think matters through.

It was perfectly natural for Cece to be impressed by a handsome young man and probably no cause for alarm at all. Perhaps it was even for the best. Cecelia had lived in a limited society all her life, and she would need to polish her public skills if she were to get along in a wider and more diverse population. Until she met her future husband, of course, Claire thought, someone considerate and appropriate, someone who could take care of Cece in the generous, loving, and kind way her sister deserved. After all, that was one of the reasons for leaving the lush warmth of India for this drab, cold country: an advantageous marriage for Cecelia, one that would ensure her sister's happiness. An innocent conversation with a future soldier was no danger to that goal and might, in fact, be a help. The clanging alarm Claire had felt at the earnest regard she had heard in Cece's voice dimmed. Really, she was becoming overly sensitive and fretful, no doubt the result of the long trip. Cecelia was a rare beauty, sweet-tempered and biddable, intelligent and loyal. Any man, Mr. Macapee included, would be delighted with her in all respects. His warm appreciation was a typical reaction to meeting Cecelia for the first time, and Cece's interested response unexceptionally normal for a young gentlewoman offered such unabashed admiration. Examining all aspects of the situation, Claire concluded that there was nothing she needed to squelch. She had appointed herself her sister's gate keeper, determined to swing open the entrance for only the right gentleman, and she was certain she would recognize the right gentleman when she saw him. Mr. Macapee, as attractive and friendly and principled as he might be, was most assuredly not that man.

Claire's first glimpse of Loden Hall was a disappointment. It was dusk when they entered the grounds and a light, cold drizzle sputtered from a depressing sky the color of pewter. When Betcher shouted down that they were coming near, Claire stuck her head outside long enough to see some great hulking stone structure looming in the distance. A prison, perhaps? An asylum? But, no, she thought with a resigned sigh, they could not be so fortunate to share the grounds with either madmen or criminals. That ominous building must certainly be Loden Hall.

Cece rearranged herself to follow her sister's example by the window and Claire said hastily, "No, no! It is too damp and cold, Cece, to peer outside. You will see the place soon enough."

Claire had quickly determined that even a distant glimpse of the dismal and dark house might bring tears to her sister's eyes. Cece did so love warmth and color! There was nothing to be done about it, of course, but Claire was vexed no end that they must greet their new home on such an unlovely and uninspiring evening.

Coming up the drive, Claire's attention was diverted from the ponderous, dark house by the unkempt grounds they passed. It's late winter, she told herself, and the ragged lawns probably cannot be helped. She thought she might also be comparing the landscape of Loden Hall to the scenery she had left behind and knew that to be an unfair study. The memory of masses of vivid rhododendrons, drifts of blue poppies that resembled the waves of an ocean, wild roses climbing with profligate abandon over doorways and walls perfuming the air with a sweet, heady fragrance would surely make the dreary winter surroundings of the Loden Valley seem even more somber by comparison.

Claire's niggling little doubt burgeoned into full alarm as soon as she stepped through the front doorway into the dark entryway of Loden Hall. No rationale, no matter how practical or firm, could hold out against her sinking feeling of foreboding. She now understood the unspoken message Symonton and his nephew had shared. No welcoming fires, no table groaning under the weight of meats and puddings waited anywhere in sight.

The four Penwarrens and one unusually quiet cat stood in the hallway with only a housekeeper introducing herself as Crayton to greet them, and she not bothering to conceal her antagonism. Claire felt Cece shiver beside her, either in response to the great stone hall, barren of decoration and damp as the inside of a well, or to the housekeeper's frigid, disdainful tone. Whatever the reason, hearing Cecelia's little gasp of dismay was all it took for Claire to find her voice and her will.

"How do you do, Mrs. Crayton? We are pleased to meet you. I am Claire Penwarren. Is our aunt available?"

"She's not feeling well. Said to tell you she'd see you in the morning," Crayton replied, both her tone and her face bland but still managing to send a distinct message for all her lack of expression. An uncomfortable silence followed.

Claire heard the housekeeper's message, which had nothing to do with the spoken words, and recognized the battle line. Crayton might as well have brandished a sword. But Cece was distressed, the boys were hungry, and Babu was on the verge of expressing his unhappiness in terms that could not be misunderstood. Sword or not, Claire had reached her limit of patience.

She took one deep and quiet breath, gave the smile that people better than Crayton had been unable to vanquish, and reaching up to untie her bonnet said, "I'm so very sorry to hear of Aunt Sophie's unhealthful disposition. Perhaps she will feel well enough to see me later in the evening, but at any event, we are thrilled to be home at last. Please direct us to the nearest fire and arrange for our bags to be brought in. Then let the kitchen know that we are all famished, including Babu, and quite willing and eager to eat whatever can be set before us as quickly as possible. I realize this may seem a terrible imposition and will express my gratitude to the cook personally as soon as I herd my family a little closer to warmth. We will take care of our own wraps, thank you, Crayton, so you needn't bother with them right now."

"Her ladyship don't hold with unnecessary fires," said Crayton. She recognized a dismissal when she heard it but felt duty-bound to resist Claire's air of cheerful authority.

"How very sensible of Aunt Sophie! I am quite in charity with such wise thrift, but, of course, we are chilled to the bone so this would hardly be an *unnecessary* fire. Our father is always one to say that a fire is just the thing for thawing both hands and conversation. Do you know our father?"

Claire met Crayton's suspicious look with an innocent one of her own. Our father the new earl, she might as well have said aloud, Philip, Lord Loden, now the owner of this monstrous building, the kitchen, the kindling, and all the fireplaces in the entire blasted place. Claire had no need to express herself so bluntly, however. A cool, pleasant smile would be period to the implied sentence. Crayton with her highly-developed instinct for self-preservation missed none of the message.

"No, Miss, I haven't had the pleasure." Crayton's manner was suddenly obsequious and smooth. She had taken Claire's measure and acknowledged defeat.

Claire recognized a vanquished opponent but did not allow time for self congratulation. Stepping down the huge hallway, she pushed open doors and peered into the side rooms until she reached one that caused her to say, "This will do. We will have our meal here, I think, and a fire immediately, please."

Later, with a roaring fire taking the chill off the room, her sister and brothers comfortably seated beside the hearth, and Babu's desultory purrs joining their murmurs of appreciation, Claire found Crayton hovering in the hallway just outside the room.

Perhaps the woman appreciated the warmth as much as they did, Claire thought, before she said, "I'll follow you to the kitchen now, Mrs. Crayton. What is the cook's name?"

"Mrs. Feastwell."

"Really?" Claire choked back a laugh. "How very apposite!"

Despite the apparent good humor of her words, the more Claire saw of their new residence, the unhappier she was with her surroundings. Every room she'd seen had appeared nearly empty and what furnishings there were seemed threadbare and shabby. Her father remembered the place much differently and from her early years had described to her a glamorous and beautiful home. While she wouldn't let her emotions show, Claire privately felt disappointed and disheartened. It was more than she really wanted to deal with this late in the day and after so lengthy a journey. She was weary and confused and longed as much as any of her siblings for a warm meal followed by a soft featherbed.

The kitchen looked as if it hadn't been refurbished in a century, and the burly woman on the other side of the old, scarred wooden table seemed to have come out of the last century, too, perhaps as royal executioner. She certainly looked as if she would like to do Claire some physical harm, arms folded across her chest and a mulish expression on her heavy face. Claire gave her a bright smile.

"How do you do, Mrs. Feastwell? I must tell you that once we reached the county's borders, we began to hear countless compliments about the kitchen at Loden Hall, which must surely be all your doing. We feel singularly fortunate to have you here. I realize our arrival is inconvenient for you so late in the day, but we would be grateful for your willingness to set us a meal. I've told Mrs. Crayton that we will eat in the library on trays to spare setting a table this evening. Tomorrow's breakfast will be soon enough for proper table manners. Tonight we will have whatever you can gather quickly—soup, bread and meat, any vegetables you can find, anything warm and filling. Tea for my sister and me, please, and something sweet for my brothers. You know boys' appetites." Absent of any patronizing or arrogant tone, there was nothing special about Claire's words, but as she spoke in a tone of friendly and grateful conspiracy, Feastwell's stolidly disapproving expression gradually softened.

No grand dame here, the cook thought with thanksgiving, just a nice young lady with two hungry brothers. By the time Claire was finished, Feastwell was already bustling around the kitchen.

"You go back up where it's warm, Miss. I'll have something brought to you before you know it. How about cream buns for the lads? I've never known a boy to refuse one of my cream buns."

"Perfect!" exclaimed Claire with the same enthusiasm she might have shown for the successful culmination of a search for the Holy Grail. "They haven't had anything even close to such a treat in three months. I knew you'd suggest just the right thing." With another smile she turned and left Crayton and Feastwell alone in the kitchen.

"Doesn't seem like what we were led to expect," Feastwell remarked tersely.

"They've only just arrived. True colors take a while to show," Crayton said in return, then gave the cook a meaningful look and went to supervise opening the bedrooms. Maybe Feastwell could be bought off with a few well-placed words and a pretty, white smile, but Crayton knew this could be the beginning of trouble. They might have to work now, really work, and Crayton wasn't at all sure she wanted to do that. It had been an easy life for quite a while and she wasn't ready to admit the need for change.

About the time the two Penwarren boys were biting into cream buns, the Most Honourable Robert Septimus Louis Carlisle, Marquis of Symonton and Baron Carlisle of several lesser regions stretched his long legs out in front of the fire in his sister's comfortable drawing room. If it could be said that Symonton was ever happy or content—a conjecture sometimes debated among his acquaintances and few friends—it would be only when he spent time with his sister. He'd had a distant affection for his late brother-in-law, Roland, Earl of Pasturson, primarily because his sister had cared so deeply for her husband, and when Roland had died suddenly in a riding accident leaving his wife with three young children and too many debts, Symonton stepped in with his usual ruthless loyalty to the few people he cared about. He settled all the debts, arranged his sister's affairs so she need not worry about her or her children's future, tried to teach young Vernon, the new Earl of Pasturson, the necessities of estate ownership, ensured Alice made a suitable match, and anticipated buying Harry a commission that would give him a future. Vernon had proved an apt pupil, if too self-important a young man for Symonton's tastes, and now stubbornly insisted that he and not their uncle be allowed to take over the cost of his younger brother's commission. For Symonton, Vernon's repeated assertions had become tiresome and Margaret, who had learned long ago to recognize the signs of her brother's deadly impatience, needed to defend her elder son without annoying her brother. Not that Robert ever acted annoyed with her, she thought fondly, no matter what terrible reputation he had in other parts of their world. He'd always been the soul of goodness to her and she would not hear him disparaged.

"I know how Vernon can be, Robert, even better than you. I bore him, after all. He has always worn the mantle of responsibility with noticeably bent shoulders but he means well. He's just too aware, as I am, that you've done more for us than any of us had the right to expect. He doesn't want you to be inconvenienced by us any longer."

Symonton raised one dark eyebrow, a disconcerting effect against his bright hair, one that made him seem satyr-like and wicked. Margaret knew he cultivated a reputation to match the look, encouraged it for his own reasons that only she grasped, and even her knowledge was imperfect. Her brother was a difficult man to understand and more difficult to get close to, but she loved him nevertheless, nine years his senior and thrilled from the beginning to have a baby brother. After the death of their mother, theirs had been a lonely childhood and the two had grown close. How he had gone from that fresh-faced and bubbly toddler to this cool-eyed, cool-hearted man she didn't know for sure and dared to speculate about it only in the privacy of her own thoughts.

"When have you ever been an inconvenience to me, Margaret?"

"I could name several occasions, but you would be bored before the end of the recitation so I'll forego the exercise. Vernon takes the responsibilities of elder son seriously and with a new wife feels them even more deeply now. He doesn't mean to be ungrateful, you know. He's actually quite fond of you." At Symonton's look she protested with a laugh, "No, really, he is. It's just that you never welcome that kind of information, so out of respect for your wishes he has stopped trying to tell you so."

Symonton thought his sister was probably right. He didn't invite words of solicitude from his family, did not want gratitude or anything even bordering on the obsequious, was not comfortable with articulated affection and on some deeper level did not trust it. He loved Margaret but never spoke of his feelings, had a strong regard for Harry, could tolerate Vernon and Alice, and that was probably the sum total of true emotion in his life. He'd grown tired of his most recent high-flyer several months before, had given her a generous farewell gift, and could no longer remember her name. Sometimes, if he thought about it at all and he seldom did, he accepted that there must be something lacking in him, an absence of the ability to feel things deeply. Perhaps he was some kind of medical oddity.

Just then Harry came into the room and dropped onto the sofa beside his mother. "Did Uncle tell you about meeting the Penwarrens today?"

Margaret looked at Symonton in reproachful surprise and said, "Not a single word." Her brother's silence and disinterested shrug compelled her to prompt, "Well?"

It was Harry who answered. "There are four of them."

"Five," corrected Symonton. "You forgot Babu."

"Babu?" repeated Margaret.

"I think he means the cat," said Harry. "A lean white thing that I understand gave my uncle quite a turn."

"How was that?" She knew of nothing that could give her brother a *turn,* the man imperturbable to the point of affectation.

Symonton gave a half smile. "I was taken to task for exaggerating the creature's effect on my livestock and warned not to mope for fear of injuring my health, so I am unwilling to utter a word of criticism or complaint."

Margaret looked helplessly at both men. "I have no idea what either of you is talking about. Are these Philip's children that have arrived? I thought he had just the one daughter."

"No," said Harry, "he has at least one other daughter." Here his tone was so reverential that his mother smiled.

"I gather that other daughter caught your attention."

"She would catch anyone's attention, gleaming black hair, dark brown eyes, and skin like coffee and cream. She looked like an Indian princess." Margaret was surprised.

"Did Philip take an Indian wife after Constance died? Loden never said a word about that."

"There were two identical twin boys, besides, and nothing foreign about them, so I gather he must have had yet a third wife. One hopes the women were consecutive and not simultaneous. Even on foreign soil that would take a toll from any husband," said Symonton easily.

"Robert," Margaret replied with laughing reproof, "don't be flippant. I'll pay a visit and meet our new neighbors so I can make my own observations, but I am sure they would appreciate time to get settled first. Poor things if they expected a warm welcome when they arrived tonight. The talk is that Sophie will make her removal as unpleasant as possible."

"That don't seem right," said Harry with a frown. "It's not their fault they inherit the place. The old Earl and his wife had plenty of time to ensure they had an heir."

"Harry!" His mother was not in the mood to discuss her neighbors' childlessness or discourse on the reasons for it, and she was not about to let her son reflect on it, either.

"Well, you know what I mean, and now that the new owners are here to take what's rightfully theirs, old Sophie ought to be dignified about doing her duty."

"Don't be disrespectful toward Lady Loden, Harry. She must leave her home of thirty years."

"You had to leave your home, too, when Vernon married Susannah," Harry pointed out, "but you didn't take a tone with anyone."

"I had this wonderful Dower House to come to, which suits me more than the big hall ever did. Lord Loden didn't follow your father's example and show the same foresight for his wife." It was the closest she would come to being critical. "Sophie has no place to go except to her brother and his wife, and there's no love lost there. She was left with nothing at her husband's death, and that's enough to make any woman bitter and fearful."

She thought privately that Sophie had been bitter and fearful long before her husband's death but did not say so aloud. Unlike her own marriage, her neighbors had had an unhappy union and Thomas Penwarren, the departed earl, had been an overbearing and autocratic husband with a way about him that often bordered on the cruel. There had been times in their company that Margaret had cringed at the tone and manner Lord Loden used with his wife.

"I thought I might ask Sophie to come and live with me for a while." The words stirred even her brother from his lethargy.

Both men sat up as if they'd been stung by insects and said, "What?!" with simultaneous horror.

"I was just thinking about it," Margaret repeated, "and it would be only for a short while until Sophie felt better about going to her brother's."

"If you follow through with that idea," Symonton told her with forbidding severity, "you will have to do without my company."

"Robert, I do without your company ten out of every twelve months as it is," his sister replied in a reasonable tone, "and I'm sure I can fit Sophie's visit around the two months of the year when you deign to join us. Besides, you said yesterday you would be leaving for London at the end of this week."

"I've changed my mind about that. If you can tolerate me, I thought I might stay on a few weeks longer."

Margaret, who was more familiar with her brother's moods than anyone else, caught some new tone in his voice and would have asked about it, but eyeing his expression she decided against another question. Something about his bored, lazy-lidded look did not invite more inquisition.

Instead, ever the doting sister, she exclaimed, "That's wonderful news! You know very well that you could stay year round if you chose. You haven't spent spring in the valley in a long time, and I think you will enjoy yourself."

"Yes," answered her brother, already losing interest in the conversation, "I think I will, too."

Chapter 3

*O*nce she assured herself that the bedrooms were safely heated and the bed linens clean, Claire said good night to her brothers and to Cecelia. The sisters had adjoining rooms, both too cavernous and dark for either of their comfort, but there was nothing to be done about that on their first night. This was home now, Claire told herself as she went in search of Crayton, and Loden Hall's transformation must be gradual and respectful to her Aunt Sophie, however much Claire might wish to rip down all the heavy window coverings and tear up the threadbare carpets first thing in the morning.

"Mrs. Crayton, I wonder if my aunt would be able to see me before I retire."

"I believe her ladyship is asleep."

"Would you find out if that is indeed true?" Claire requested, not giving ground. "I'll wait here until you return. If her health will not allow her to see me this evening, please extend my sympathy and tell her I will look forward to greeting her at breakfast." Claire wasn't surprised at the answer Crayton brought back.

"Her ladyship begs your pardon and your understanding but she says that talking makes her head ache. She hopes she'll feel better by morning."

With Crayton's slight emphasis on *hopes*, Claire heard her aunt's intended message clearly and sighed. Everything was always such a struggle. Why couldn't people interact with a modicum of good sense and good manners and just get along? Of course, she understood that her Aunt Sophie thought she was going to be dispossessed of her home and felt resentful and angry about it. That was perfectly understandable, but to take this pouting, punishing approach to a situation that was hardly anyone's fault—except her Uncle Thomas's, perhaps, for dying so precipitously—made no sense. Life itself sometimes didn't make sense, but for Claire, possessed of an orderly and organized temperament, there was always a way to set things right without being reduced to rudeness or any kind of emotional outburst.

After peeking into the room directly across the hall to assure herself that her brothers were soundly asleep, Claire decided she could not stay awake one more moment. She went into her room, admired Babu as he lay with his nose tucked under both paws at the foot of her bed, and wished she had remembered to ask Cece's help getting out of her gown. There were small buttons front and back and every single one of them a nuisance. All her garments, night clothes included, were still packed in their traveling trunk because Crayton was not going to do anything without being asked—something that will change, Claire thought grimly as she rummaged for a nightdress, and sooner rather than later—and Claire had finally dug out something serviceable when she heard muffled sounds from the adjoining room. She pulled her nightdress over her head and stood motionless, shocked at what the sounds meant, before she went over to knock lightly at the door.

"Cece?"

The sounds ceased and a soft voice spoke. "Yes?"

Claire pushed the door fully open and went through to stand at the foot of the bed. Light from Claire's room illumined her sister's form huddled under the covers.

"Are you crying?" Claire asked, both dismay and surprise coloring her words.

At first, Cecelia didn't answer. Finally in the same soft voice that caught on the smallest of sobs she said, "I'm sorry, Claire. I didn't mean for you to hear. You have enough to worry about without my foolishness." Her tone was so humble and so forlorn that Claire was by her sister's side in a moment.

"Oh, Cece, I know it's been awful for you, everything so strange and cold and dark, but it will get better! I promise."

Cecelia started to say something but couldn't finish because she had begun to cry in earnest, silently, with her hand pressed over her mouth, her mute shudders pronounced enough that the mound of blankets over her shook, too.

Claire looked at her sister helplessly, so affected by the sight of her sweet-natured sister distraught and weeping that at first she couldn't think what to say or do. At last rallied by a surge of fierce protectiveness, she crawled into bed beside Cecelia and gathered her into her arms.

"I promise," Claire repeated. "I promise it will be all right. You'll see. Please don't cry." Claire was the mother again, as she'd been from the beginning, as proud and protective and tender as her beautiful Indian stepmother, who had died giving birth to Cecelia. Cece was always so resolutely quiet and pleasant, so tractable, never one to complain or weep, that the presence of tears moved and horrified her sister. To feel Cecelia trembling—whether from cold or fatigue or fear Claire couldn't tell—troubled her more than anything else had on the entire trip.

"I miss Papa," said Cece, sounding ten instead of twenty. "I'm just tired, Claire. Please forgive me. I wouldn't add to your burdens for all the world." Slowly the warmth of the fire and her sister's embrace began to calm Cecelia's shivering. "This is like when we were little girls. Remember, Claire, when I thought I heard some creature slither into my room but was afraid to make a sound? You heard me whimpering and stormed in with a stool you'd snatched from somewhere. I remember how you looked in the moonlight creeping from corner to corner with the stool aimed in front of you as if you expected you'd have to hold off a lion. Your face was so intense and so fierce that I became frightened for you and cried even more. I was sure something terrible was going to happen to you."

"Yes," said Claire, her sister's head now buried in her shoulder and the sound of tears gone, "I remember. You wouldn't let me leave the room so I crawled in with you until morning. How can you recall that incident? You couldn't have been older than three at the time."

"You are the best of sisters," murmured Cece in drowsy tones, "and I remember much more than you give me credit for."

Claire started to speak but knew from Cece's deep breathing and relaxed muscles that her sister had fallen asleep. She gave thought to throwing back the covers and padding to her own room but fell asleep, too, and slumbered soundly until daylight cracked through the heavy curtains.

When Claire awoke, she experienced a rather frightening moment when she couldn't recall where she was, but she saw her sister's beautiful, sleeping profile next to her, looked around the room that seemed even drabber by daylight, and remembered everything—the arduous voyage, the cold carriage ride, the forbidding hall they must now call home, Crayton and Feastwell and her Aunt Sophie hiding in her bed chamber. Everything. She was mistress of Loden Hall with work to be done, battles to be fought, and changes to be made. Claire was not about to have her sister cry herself to sleep one more night. Like a knight armed for tournament, she swung both feet firmly onto the cold floor, carefully rearranged the covers over the still sleeping Cecelia, and padded on slippered feet into her own room to dress for the day. No hot water waiting, she thought, and added it to the list of things that must change, although to be fair she knew it was unfashionably early for the household to be up and about.

Claire loved mornings, the time of the day when she felt clear-headed and unencumbered by past problems, and thought she did her best work when the day was fresh. Her father had taught her to believe that every day was an opportunity, that only her own fears and doubts could keep her from success, and most of the time Claire was inclined to believe her father's counsel. She could recall one or two rare circumstances when she had felt overwhelmed and briefly weepy and she kept those few occasions to herself. This first day in their new home Claire, with her typical self-confidence, experienced only one emotion: determination. Those who knew Claire well would have read it on her face, would have recognized purpose in the tilt of her head and the direct challenge of her gaze. Not just battle ready. Battle hungry.

Once dressed and ready for the day—making another mental note to enlist a lady's maid for her sister and herself—Claire found her way to the kitchen.

"Good morning, Mrs. Feastwell. I hope you had a pleasant night. My brothers are still abed, no doubt dreaming of your cream buns. They were just the thing."

The cook, who at this second meeting decided she wanted to be Miss Penwarren's cook for all her life if only that could be arranged, replied, "That's kind of you to say, Lady Claire," and swelled a little with pride, reminding Claire with sudden and disconcerting memory of the peahens that had wandered the lawns in India.

"I'm not accustomed to Lady Claire, Mrs. Feastwell; plain Miss Claire will do just fine for the household. May we have breakfast around ten and is there a morning room?" At the cook's nod, Claire added, "Then if you'll lay breakfast there, I promise to have appreciative appetites ready for it. Is Mrs. Crayton about?"

"I'm sure I couldn't say." Thinking her tone might have sounded disrespectful, Feastwell hastily added, "Crayton keeps her own schedule, Miss, and I've yet to figure it out. Not that I mean to speak out of school."

"Of course, not. I'll find her. If you should see her first, I would appreciate it if you would ask her to seek me out. Are there others who help in the house?"

"Most were let go when the master died, like Mr. Steepen, the butler, and 'most all the day girls, too. Crayton and I were retained, Betcher kept for the stables, and there's little Moira that tries to keep up with the house. She's a good girl but just one, after all, and she can only do so much."

"Where would I find Moira now?"

"I'd guess cleaning out the fireplace in the library from last night."

Claire did find Moira in the library, the room where the family had dined the evening before. A slight girl knelt in front of the hearth with her back to the door, holding a small broom in one thin hand and a bucket in the other.

"You must be Moira." Claire stepped into the room, missing nothing about the servant, not her pale, peaked face with its sprinkle of red freckles, not her broken nails, not her patched apron or the dull tips of very worn shoes that peeked from under a skirt with a frayed hem.

The girl, barely past childhood, stood hastily, cap askew and a streak of soot across one cheek.

"Yes, ma'am, I am." She seemed very small, hardly taller than Will, and too thin for Claire's comfort.

"I'm Miss Penwarren, Moira. You'll end up calling me Miss Claire, I hope. My family and I used the fire in here last evening so thank you for being so quick to clean it. I wonder if you could show me where the morning room is."

Moira was small in stature but possessed of a quick mind and keen intuition. She took in Claire all at once, a tall, slim woman with a true smile and warm eyes, not youthful exactly but not the coldly demanding older woman Crayton had described from the night before, either. She should know by now not to trust Crayton, who had her own opinions and none of them to be believed. Moira gave an awkward curtsy.

"How do you do, Miss Claire? I'd be happy to show you the morning room. It's this way."

The breakfast room was really quite pretty, Claire thought, with large windows letting in—besides drafts—great splashes of cheerful early morning sunlight that pooled across the table and floor and brightened the whole room.

"How lovely! Will you start a fire in here, please, Moira? This is where we'll breakfast every day, and we will want to have the chill gone before we gather."

That would be a welcome change, the servant girl thought, used to working in rooms so cold her fingers went numb before she ever finished her chores.

As Moira turned to leave, Claire asked, "Have you breakfasted yourself, Moira?"

The girl, at first struck dumb by an inquiry about her own well-being, finally managed to stammer out, "No, ma'am. I'm up even before Mrs. Feastwell, and I don't usually get anything until luncheon."

Claire did not allow her displeasure with the information to color either her tone or her expression. Instead, she directed cheerfully, "Stop by the kitchen after you get this fire blazing and tell Mrs. Feastwell I ordered you to have something to eat. I know doing so may throw your morning schedule off, and I hope you'll forgive me for that." Claire exited past Moira, leaving the girl to stare after her.

Later, looking up from her toast, oatmeal, and tea Moira asked, "Do you think this is too good to be true, then?"

In answer, Feastwell, having a wish but no certain answer, only shrugged.

Aunt Sophie had not made an appearance by the time all the Penwarrens had finished breakfast, and Claire was well aware that if she weren't careful, the first skirmish would go to her aunt. She would have to take action if she were not to lose the entire war, but there was so much to be done that the need to placate a relative who should have had better manners was so frustrating that Claire could have screamed from exasperation.

Instead of screaming, however—never a justifiable action in Claire's opinion, regardless of the provocation—she poured herself another cup of coffee and stated calmly, "I'll need everyone's help today, so Will and Matt, you may take some time to go bother Betcher in the stables but be back within the hour. There's little enough sun as it is and I can't tolerate that it's hidden behind grimy windows." The boys, who knew when Claire could be argued out of work and when she couldn't, nodded obediently and were gone in an instant, leaving the sisters seated across from each other at the table.

"How unfortunate that Aunt Sophie must remain indisposed!" commented Cecelia softly, recognizing the signs of impatience in her sister that no one else might have detected. Claire would never show her annoyance in word or action but it was there to be sure, and Cecelia knew her own calm manner possessed an inherent ability to quiet and control Claire's more forceful tendencies.

Claire was on the verge of making an indiscreet response about her reclusive relative when she looked up to see a woman standing in the doorway. Aunt Sophie after all, she thought with relief, and got up hastily, saying, "You must be Aunt Sophie. I was so sorry to hear that you were indisposed with a headache last evening!"

Claire, taller than her aunt, bent to drop a kiss on the woman's dry cheek and felt her turn her cheek away and pull back so abruptly that Claire might have carried plague.

Worse than I imagined, thought Claire, but she said aloud in a pleasantly solicitous voice, "I do hope you're feeling better, Aunt. Would some hot coffee help?"

The displaced Lady Loden stared at Claire without softening or smile. She was dressed in severe black, had stiff, steel-gray hair, eyes of an indeterminate brown, a permanently lined forehead, and deep furrows that drew down the corners of her mouth in repose. Her expression seemed permanently disapproving, but Claire thought it was more than that. She had never met a woman who so radiated misery and resentment and who, despite her attempted camouflage, so reeked of fear. For all the irritation she had felt at her aunt's bad manners—Claire now recalled her own personal annoyance with regret—and regardless of the woman's forbidding exterior, Claire felt a quick and real sympathy for her aunt. What kind of a sad, unhappy life was etched across the woman's face?

"Forgive me for my presumption. I should have introduced myself first. I'm Claire, and this is my sister, Cecelia. My brothers, Matthew and William, like boys will, have already breakfasted and are exploring outside." Cecelia came forward to stand next to Claire.

"Hello, Aunt Sophie. I'm very pleased to meet you." Like Claire, Cecelia brushed the woman's cheek with a soft kiss.

Claire took the older woman by her rigid arm and brought her forward to the table, saying as she did so, "We've set a place for you by the window; the sunlight is so welcome after yesterday's gloom. We're very glad you felt well enough to join us." She supposed the role of hostess still properly belonged to her aunt, but the woman had shown neither propensity nor desire for the task, and perhaps it was best that they all take their new roles in the house as quickly as possible without a lot of fuss and ceremony

"The sunlight," replied Sophie by way of greeting her nieces, "makes my head ache." Cecelia went immediately to draw the curtains as Claire pulled back a chair.

"Of course, it does. I should have realized. Let Cece bring you coffee and a slice of toast. I'm convinced you will feel better with a little nourishment."

Despite her intention to be unaccommodating and unresponsive, Sophie Penwarren soon found herself sitting across from her nieces sipping coffee and being offered buttered toast as if she were still lady of the hall. Her hall, her home for so many years, and now usurped. Well, she would eat with them but she drew the line at making polite conversation.

"We were so sorry to hear of Uncle Thomas's death," Claire said as she spooned marmalade onto her aunt's toast. "Being so far away, the news was terribly delayed but I trust you received our sincere condolences." Claire paused with the spoon mid-air to raise her eyebrows inquiringly and allow her poised and patient silence time to compel a response from her aunt. As always, the ploy was successful.

"Yes. Thank you." Sophie snipped out the words of token courtesy and then concentrated on her plate as the two young women chatted softly between themselves. They were well bred at any rate, Sophie thought, even the foreign-looking one. If she must be displaced, at least it was by someone with pretty manners that wouldn't shame what was left of the family's good name.

After a while there was only quiet in the room. Claire, determined to have conversation, put a small smile on her face and watched her aunt intermittently but without speaking. Cecelia looked down at her hands folded in her lap as if she were praying. The drawn-out quiet eventually had its desired effect.

"I suppose," Sophie said, each word clipped and precise, "that you are wondering when I plan to leave."

"No, I can't say that we were wondering anything of the sort," responded Claire, but her aunt continued undeterred as if she had rehearsed a speech from which she would not deviate whatever the interruption. And perhaps she had done exactly that, Claire thought, observing how the lines of the woman's face deepened with the effort of speaking.

"Naturally, if I'd known exactly when you planned to arrive, I would have already departed so as not to be an encumbrance for you. My brother and his wife are very anxious for me to come to them. Very anxious. But in good conscience I felt I could not allow you to arrive at a house empty of welcome. That would hardly have ensured an appropriate reception for you." If Sophie recognized the irony of her words, considering the dark, cold house and her own absence of the night before, it didn't show. "Now that you're here, I can be gone by the end of the week. I hope," her harsh voice quavered for one imperceptible moment, "that will be to your convenience, unless you wish me gone sooner."

"We don't wish you gone at all," responded Claire with amiable calm, "and certainly not by the end of the week." She paused with a smile. "Unless you are so eager to be with your brother and his wife that you feel you must abandon us that quickly. We would understand, of course, but we would be desolate."

Sophie stopped with the piece of toast midway to her lips, frozen for a moment into confused immobility. All she could croak out was, "I beg your pardon."

"Dear Aunt Sophie," said Claire, "we would be thrilled if you would choose to stay on with us, at least for a while. Papa will join us in the summer and he expressly asked me to plead that you stay with us until he arrives. I realize there may be a certain awkwardness in this situation, and we wouldn't make you uncomfortable for the world, but please say you will stay into the summer, at least. Father would consider it the kindest of gestures on your part and would be so grateful. Indeed, we would all be grateful. Surely your brother will understand."

He'll turn somersaults, thought Sophie, and his wife will do handsprings, but she said to Claire with becoming concession, "Of course, if I can be of any modest assistance to you, I will stay. I'll write my brother and explain. He's sure to understand the demands of family obligation." He understands family obligation only too well, she thought, and will be thrilled to be relieved of his.

"How wonderful!" said Cecelia, finally raising her gaze from her lap. Sophie looked at the girl with suspicion, thinking there must be some mockery there, but there didn't look to be. Those limpid almost black eyes smiled right at her. Claire, too, was smiling over the rim of her cup.

"You know, Aunt, this has been your home for so many years, we will need your advice on how to proceed. Would your health allow you to show us around the hall this morning? We saw only the library and our bedrooms last night."

So Sophie, prepared to schedule her departure and sure of a superior farewell from her successors, found herself instead giving a walking tour of Loden Hall, followed by one white cat that condescended his company and four Penwarrens who hung on every word she spoke and made just the right response at the right time to her every comment. Except for the twins, that is, whose attention wandered more often than not and who showed no particular interest in Georgian architecture or French fabrics. Still, they were just boys and could be forgiven a lack of interest, even if the older one—Will? Matt? Sophie vowed to get them straight in her mind—would one day own everything he saw, whether he was interested in its history or not.

It soon became evident that there was not much to be said about the furnishings or the fabrics, from whatever part of the globe they may have originated, because there simply weren't many of either to talk about. The boys had raced on ahead to their assigned window washing tasks and Cecelia followed her brothers at a more decorous pace when Sophie stopped and put her hand on Claire's arm to keep her from following her siblings, the familiar gesture a far cry, thought Claire with satisfaction, from the morning's recoil.

"I suppose," said Sophie without preamble, "that you wonder why there are so few furnishings. I wouldn't want you to think that in some scandalous and improper way I took advantage of your absence to profit from their sale."

"Such an idea never crossed my mind, Aunt."

For the first time that day the older woman seemed uncomfortable and unsure of herself. Her words came out halting.

"The truth is that your Uncle Thomas had a sincere, but unfortunate and often misguided, predilection for wine and horses. He was also the unluckiest man in the county. That combination caused a slow decimation of the house's furnishings. It was his house, after all, and he could do as he pleased with it." Following that mandatory defense, Sophie added, "I hope you understand."

Oh, yes, thought Claire, who with those words at last made sense of both the house's and her aunt's appearance, I understand very well. She also astutely guessed that wine and gambling may not have been her uncle's only indulgences, and while she would certainly never embarrass her aunt by pursuing that particular subject, Claire could finally account for the bitter unhappiness that colored every aspect of her Aunt Sophie's deportment.

Aloud Claire remarked, "I see. Papa must have inherited all the luck in the family, then. His venture into tea is very successful, and we were quite fortunate that from his arrival in India he was able to establish a flourishing and profitable enterprise." She tucked her aunt's hand under her arm and walked slowly with her down the steps. "I'm relieved that you brought up the subject, Aunt Sophie, and please forgive me in advance if I overstep, but in the face of your shared confidence, may I assume you will not be offended if I make some small effort to refurbish the house? Papa will be here this summer and I would so like it to be as he remembers." At the foot of the steps Sophie stopped to face her niece.

"There's no money in the estate, girl. Surely you realize that."

"Yes, I do realize that, but Papa had the thoughtful foresight to set aside monies for whatever purposes I find necessary. He trusts my judgment completely, and I think creating a comfortable home would please him no end."

"My dear Claire, it will take a great deal of money to do what you suggest."

"My dear Aunt Sophie," said Claire, once more taking her aunt's arm and resuming their stroll, "forgive me if I sound vulgar, but we have a great deal of money."

****

At the end of a fortnight when Lady Pasturson announced that she intended to call on the Penwarrens, she was astonished to hear her brother volunteer to join her.

"Robert," Margaret protested, "you can't want to spend your afternoon with chattering females, especially when one of them is Sophie Penwarren. You've never been able to tolerate her." He didn't disagree but qualified her comments.

"I disliked her husband long before I disliked her, and I have one or two vague memories of almost feeling sorry for the woman. Fortunately the emotion passed without doing any lasting damage. I assure you I will tolerate her presence with the greatest good temper."

Harry, listening, exclaimed, "Ha!" followed it with a laugh, and then added unashamedly, "Really, Uncle, good temper might have been acceptable but *greatest* good temper overreaches." Symonton cuffed his nephew with lazy affection.

"Be quiet, pup. I can be on good behavior when I choose. The problem is that I so seldom feel the desire to do so."

"Well, I must see this, so I'm coming, too," Harry declared, adding with attractive meekness, "As long as you don't mind, Mother."

Margaret understood her son's desire to see an attractive female again, but her brother's willingness to visit the new neighbors was an incomprehensible offer. In all the years he'd been coming to the Loden Valley, Robert had never once shown anything but the strongest aversion to hobnobbing with the locals. He seemed always out of place in her neighbors' country drawing rooms, supremely self-confident, slightly scornful, and hovering at the edge of impropriety. She knew he acted so on purpose and seemed to enjoy any discomfort or outrage he left in his wake, and she felt a brief hesitation to take her brother with her. It was not the welcome she desired for two delicately bred young women, and Sophie's bad temper aside, the woman had lost her husband and was losing her home. Surely she deserved a little kindness and understanding.

Well aware of her hesitation and the reason for it, Symonton said, "Really, Margaret, you have my word. I won't embarrass you." Such rare humility won her over and that afternoon all three stood on the doorstep of Loden Hall.

A young woman in crisp dress and cap answered the door, bobbed a greeting, took their cards, and ushered them into the hallway. Margaret looked around her in amazement. How could anything have changed so radically in such a short space of time? When she'd last called on Sophie, the hulking house had been all damp and dust, but now the smell of lemon oil and beeswax was everywhere, doorways reflected the glow of well-polished wood, walls were stripped of dirt and soot, and the smell of paint came from somewhere distant. Really, now that she thought of it, had the entranceway always been papered in attractive swirls of spring green?

The place held the bustle and air of concentrated activity, besides. Two chattering girls in servants' dress stepped quickly up the stairs with their arms full of linens and from somewhere distant she heard a boy shouting, "No fair, Will, no fair! You had a head start!" It had never been like this ever in her memory, not even when Thomas was alive, perhaps *especially* when Thomas was alive. The three visitors stood just inside the door, all of them, even Symonton, bemused by the change, when their attention was caught by the young woman walking briskly down the hallway toward them.

What a wonderful face, thought Margaret. None of its parts were particularly exceptional, but the sparkling hazel eyes, thick auburn hair, patrician nose, rosy complexion, and wide, warm smile formed a picture so welcoming and so attractive in total that you felt there was no one with whom you would rather spend time and no better, warmer place than right here to spend it. This must be Claire, the older sister.

"Hello, Lady Pasturson, how very kind of you to visit! We should have done so eventually but to have you come to us first is such an honor. I'm Claire Penwarren. I believe I've had the pleasure of meeting these gentlemen already. Will you let Mrs. Crayton take your things and join me in the drawing room? I hope you can forgive all the hubbub. Mrs. Crayton has enlisted the help of girls from the village since I found the tradition of spring housecleaning too strong to resist." Through all this convivial speech, Claire helped hand coats and hats to Crayton, then placed a respectful hand on Margaret's arm and steered her without force or obvious insistence into a side room. Watching her, Symonton knew a quick admiration as one social professional to another. She was as smooth as he when he chose to put himself out to play society's game, and that was the highest praise he could offer.

"Aunt Sophie is on her way and my sister Cecelia, also. They were deciding patterns and colors for the upstairs bedchambers. How fortunate that our Aunt Sophie has such good taste!" The room in which they stood reflected nothing of Sophie's taste, thought Symonton, and everything of the woman's standing before them. The walls had been painted in sapphire blue, and new window coverings of sky blue and white coordinated well with the soft, striped, recently upholstered furniture. From somewhere she had managed to dig up two classic end tables upon which stood vases of dried grasses that should have looked ridiculous but instead seemed charming. If she weren't careful, she would start a faddish practice and people everywhere would be plucking weeds to use as dinner centerpieces.

"You'll recall my son, Harry Macapee," Margaret was saying, "and my brother, Lord Symonton."

"Mr. Macapee, I'm glad to have the opportunity to restate my gratitude for your recent kind company to my sister. She was so chilled, and I had been forced to leave her on her own while I—" Claire stopped abruptly, remembering the quest for fish that had forced her to leave Cece alone, remembering, too, the hungry cat that had precipitated the search, the loosened collar, the streak of white, the rearing horses. Too late, Claire realized she should have taken her gratitude in a different direction.

Symonton watched the quick progression of memory flit faintly across Claire's expression, and when he was sure she had reached the same mental place at which he had already arrived completed her sentence for her.

"While you allowed devil cat to risk my life and limb." Claire had to laugh at his words.

"Since you will insist on believing that either Babu or I— or perhaps both of us in some kind of devious conspiracy— contrived to interrupt your travels on purpose, my lord, I will not bother with a denial, but I can assure you of my innocent intent. If you are very respectful, I might be able to convince Babu to condescend to pay you a visit, and you could then more properly berate him instead of me. I might add that Babu's intentions are always suspect and he should be reprimanded on a regular basis, regardless of any unremarkable conduct at the time."

"Since I am persuaded that any scolding of mine would have the same lack of effect on both of you, I'll forego your invitation and the pleasure of devil cat's company."

Margaret looked at her brother quickly, something in his tone giving her momentary pause. She could not recall hearing him that genuinely and naturally engaged in a conversation with a woman in years, nothing drawling or flattering or remotely patronizing about him, no bored glance or raised brow or any of the other myriad ways he had of ruthlessly displaying an aloof disdain for the company or the occasion.

At that moment Sophie entered the room and Margaret experienced another surprise. The older woman had replaced the funereal black dress she'd worn for months with one of dove gray and she looked almost—could it be?—happy. There seemed to be something resembling a smile on Sophie's face as she came forward, but that may have been a trick played by the abundance of light in the room. She was not accustomed to seeing Sophie exposed by sunlight.

"Margaret, I was just thinking how to introduce my nieces to my neighbors and here you are to help me do just that. Glad you've brought Harry and Symonton with you. Wouldn't have expected to have both gentlemen calling."

"Yes," murmured Claire, "like Portia, I feel twice blessed," and she shot Symonton a mischievous glance before offering, "Aunt, I'll go request refreshments now that you're here to entertain. Did you leave Cecelia upstairs?"

"No, I'm here," said a low voice. There was a soft, collective intake of breath from the three visitors as they looked at Cecelia framed in the doorway.

It was clear why her son had become so quickly enamored with the younger sister, thought Margaret. The girl was an exquisite, exotic vision. Everything about her was perfect, her creamy skin the color of light coffee, shining black hair, thickly lashed dark eyes, a rich red mouth, and teeth so white they seemed to glow. Of medium height, her figure was generous without being vulgar, her posture elegant, her bearing graceful. Cecelia wore a dress of natural wool in a soft beige ivory with a delicate lace collar a shade lighter at her throat. She was an extraordinarily beautiful young woman, not the typical fashionable English miss all pale and pastel but something infinitely more memorable and striking, and sure to take London by storm when the *ton* got its first glimpse of her.

Claire, aware of her guests' reverential reaction to Cecelia's entrance, smiled with pride. She loved it when people admired her sister, and they had yet to discover Cece's unselfish and kind nature, which added all the more to her attractions. Claire became conscious that Symonton had transferred his attention from Cece to her, had, in fact, fixed his gaze on her face as intently as Harry stared at Cece, although not with Harry's same enraptured esteem that bordered on worship. Instead, Symonton examined Claire with a searching and almost perplexed curiosity. She didn't know what to make of his look and decided not to spend time trying to decipher it. Her experience with the peerage and with men of fashion was limited, and she supposed she would have to improve on that deficiency before Cece came out to society, but since Symonton was not fixed on Cecelia with any look at all, Claire forgot about his reaction before she ever reached the kitchen.

She returned to a room abuzz with conversation. Aunt Sophie and Lady Pasturson were caught up in reminiscence, both women smiling, and Harry was prompting Cece to talk about her trip. Cece looked happy, Claire thought, her sister's dark eyes sparkling and her tone energetic and enthused. Claire felt mixed emotions at the sight. Remembering Cece's earlier tears, she was pleased that someone could make her sister bubble, but Claire felt a frisson of worry, too, at the happiness she saw on Cece's face. Harry Macapee was the second son of an earl and was destined for the military, nothing about him even remotely close to the advantageous matrimonial match she desired for her sister. Cecelia should have a kind and attentive husband, perhaps a little older—but certainly not to the advanced age of Symonton—and of independent means. He needn't have a title—Claire was no snob, after all—but he must be of impeccable reputation and able to give Cecelia a worry-free life. Her sister was very dear to her, and Claire had set her heart years ago on arranging Cece's perfect marriage. The life of a soldier's wife was absolutely and definitely out of the question.

Sometime in Claire's absence the twins had managed to show up and now sat one on each side of Symonton, listening to whatever he said as if he were the Buddha. When Claire stepped inside the room, her aunt looked up and patted the seat next to her.

"Come here, Claire, and tell Lady Pasturson about your voyage." With a smile, Claire went obediently to her aunt's side.

Seeing that exchange, Margaret could only marvel. Sophie was still stiff and perhaps she would never lose those lines of unhappiness that crisscrossed her face, but she looked as happy as she had ever been in all the years the two women had been neighbors. Margaret was glad of the change.

"I'm not to leave," Sophie had confided to Margaret before Claire reappeared from the kitchen. "They want me to stay, at least into the summer when their father arrives from India and perhaps longer. They're all good children, besides, even Cecelia, who at first was too foreign for my taste. But she's a quiet, well-mannered girl and very solicitous for my comfort. I can't think how that rascal Philip ended up with such an acceptable family. I'm sure none of us thought he'd amount to anything."

Claire's requested description of her trip was interrupted by two things: a great simultaneous shout of laughter from her brothers and Crayton's entrance with the tea cart. Claire stood to move to her place by the refreshments but stopped by her brothers on the way.

"I hope the boys are not a complete bore for you, my lord."

"Nothing of the sort," Symonton answered, surprised to find the words true.

"Really, Claire, we're on our best behavior," protested Matt, "only you should hear about Lord Symonton's racing. He said he once won a wager because the other fellow tried to take a shortcut and instead ended up in the middle of a fishing pond. Serves him right, I say, for not trying to win fair and square."

"I'm not sure what to make of the wager part," Claire commented to Matt, no change in her tone when she spoke but somehow managing to express a disapproval of gambling just the same, "but I agree with you completely on the other. It's no good winning if it can't be done honestly. Now come and help yourself to cakes and leave poor Lord Symonton to recover from all your pestering." After they'd gone, she said to Symonton with a smile, "It's very good of you to regale them with your past adventures."

"I fear that not all of my past adventures would be fit for young ears, but I'm careful in my selection."

"I trust your discretion, Lord Symonton, as much as I trust in the existence of your colorful past. My brothers miss their papa very much, and all my poor efforts to stand in his stead, while well intended, are just not the same. They miss the presence of a man in their lives and will hold on to you closer than shadows as long as you let them. Feel free to scoot them away if they become trying."

"My sister will tell you that I am never shy about doing exactly that, even with adults."

"Oh, especially with adults, I should say," retorted Claire, "so let me excuse myself before you are forced to scoot me away with a few well chosen words."

Later, their social call completed with a quiet return carriage ride, the three visitors once more settled themselves at home.

"I am quite breathless from that experience, and it will take me some time to recover," Margaret remarked thoughtfully. She had several matters to consider, all of them connected in some way with the effect of the Penwarrens on her own family but none of which she intended to mention to either her son or her brother.

"Yes," agreed Harry, "I feel exactly the same," a vision of dark eyes and a glowing smile still enchanting him.

Symonton remained mute, not ready to agree with Margaret or with Harry but conscious that something had changed for him and aware that if he were not careful, he might need some recovery time of his own.

Chapter 4

*F*rom her first week in her new home, Claire had resumed her habit of an early morning outing. Initially she used the time to explore the grounds and the out buildings of Loden Hall, discovering without undue surprise that the stables were in much better shape than the house. Her late uncle had apparently had no appreciation for fine art or graceful furniture, but he'd considered himself an expert at judging horseflesh, both on and off the racetrack. After his death, her aunt had somehow been able to keep creditors away from the stables and several good mounts remained. Claire had every confidence in Betcher's skill with the reins and felt no reluctance trusting him with the stock and more importantly, with her brothers. The man knew his way around horses, and when she approached him about improving her brothers' saddle skills, he was enthusiastic in his response.

"They're good boys, those brothers of yours, but for all their eagerness I can see they need more training. I'd be happy to take them on."

Everyone was agreeable, especially the twins, who couldn't believe their good fortune at having their pick of mounts. It was inexplicable to them that neither of their sisters took advantage of the well-stocked stables.

Cecelia rode respectably but didn't enjoy it, favoring less physical pastimes, and after the first week Claire discovered that she preferred a walk to a ride. She was a competent and fearless horsewoman, but her tendency for speed in the saddle kept her from appreciating the small pleasures of the Sussex countryside. The glories of the season were best appreciated with both feet on the ground. All around Claire, the Loden Valley seemed to be turning March-green. Trees showed tender light green leaves; sheep contentedly munched emerald grass; small wild creatures peered at her from under bushes suddenly plump with pale green shoots. Birds serenaded her with springtime tunes she had yet to learn. Claire had spent the last twenty-two years in India with only her father's memories of England as encyclopedia and while she had at first been disappointed with the countryside's late-winter bleakness, the lush promise of early spring that began to emerge around her was more glorious than he had described or she had imagined. Everything smelled fresh, besides, and there was a bracing coolness to the air that had never been present in India, even in the north country. So Claire rose at her usual early hour every morning, pulled on stout walking shoes and an old woolen cape, tied her hair back with a kerchief and walking stick in hand, began to explore the West Sussex hills. It was a rare time of quiet for her, a time for contemplation and devotion, a time to think and plan, to be wholly alone and unencumbered. A time to be observed and studied, too, but she was a woman of active temperament and remained unaware of her passive role in those latter pastimes.

Soon after Lady Pasturson's visit, Claire was in the middle of an early morning walk, deep in thought about her father's arrival and what that would mean for all of them, when she spied a rider in the distant east. He had pulled up atop a ridge and sat looking very clearly, very specifically, in her direction. Then he spurred forward and she recognized Symonton. Claire came to a standstill in the middle of the worn path and waited until he was close enough to hear.

"Good morning," she called, shielding her eyes as she looked up at Symonton, who had cantered forward and now sat before her on a mount as distinctive in appearance as the man. The gleaming silver gray stallion with black mane and tail looked powerful and if Claire was to judge by the proud throw of the creature's head, equally as temperamental and arrogant as its rider. "What a beautiful beast!"

"The horse you mean?" She swallowed a laugh.

"You know very well I meant the horse. A magnificent specimen!" She paused deliberately. "The horse, I mean."

That brought a smile from him. "His name is Bonaparte because he has a conceit the size of France." Changing the topic abruptly Symonton observed, "You're out and about early."

"At home in India," Claire explained, not catching her use of the word although Symonton noticed and filed it away for future reference, "I learned to walk in the early morning hours from necessity. Much of the year the midmorning heat grew too stifling to do anything out of doors, so if I wanted a walk—and I almost always did—I needed to take it before the sun rose. It was the only time I had to myself, besides, and I came to treasure the solitude."

"Is that a poorly veiled hint for me to leave you alone?"

"Not at all! When I want to be left alone I am usually quite forthright about making my wish known and seldom need to resort to mere hints, poorly veiled or otherwise. No, your company's welcome, but I'd appreciate it on my level. If I continue to stand looking up at you in this awkward manner, my neck will stiffen permanently into this posture and I will be able to converse only with people willing to position themselves on the roof of the Hall, which you'll own is hardly an acceptable way to exchange pleasantries with one's neighbors."

Symonton slid off Bonaparte and holding the reins began to walk with Claire.

"Sussex must be quite a change for you. What do you think of your new home?"

"It's beautiful," Claire responded warmly. "Papa told me often enough how richly green it was, sparkling like an emerald, he would say, but I admit I had my doubts at first. Now it seems to have changed to jewel colors practically overnight." She paused before asking with unexpected diffidence, "Please forgive my ignorance about England's geography, but is Symonton in West Sussex, too?"

"No, it's on the Cornish coast, I'm afraid."

"Why *afraid*?"

"Cornwall has a beauty all its own but nothing so verdantly English as Sussex. In fact, there are many that consider Cornwall to be one of the most desolate and lonely places in the Empire. Symonton Manor sits close enough to the ocean that on a windy day sea spray splashes against the library windows. No matter where you are in the house, and it's half again the size of Loden Hall, you can hear the constant pounding of the surf. Margaret always felt the isolation, and I think she appreciated the move to this gentler climate when she married."

"But I think you prefer Cornwall to Sussex, my lord."

"Unless you're uncomfortable with it, I wish you'd call me Symonton, and yes, I do prefer the coast to the valley. I don't know why."

She threw him a quick sidelong glance before saying in a matter-of-fact tone, "Nonsense. Of course, you know why. Not for you the mundane or the mild. You're too easily bored and if you spent too long surrounded by this peaceful green paradise, you'd go mad. Next thing we'd hear is that you were running wild through town on Bonaparte, pistols drawn and shouting out some brazen challenge to the authorities to come and get you. I can picture the scene now. Frankly, I'd be surprised if you spent longer than a month here at any given stretch. It's your nature to prefer the pounding ocean to this green valley, no matter how lovely it is."

Symonton had halted midway through Claire's observations, but she didn't realize it until she'd walked a few brisk steps ahead, concluded her comments, waited for a response from him that did not come, and finally turned around to look for him.

"What is it?" she asked, somewhat bemused by the way he stood in the middle of the lane looking at her—glaring, really—as if she'd suddenly sprouted wings. Or horns, more likely, Claire thought with amusement, trying to gauge the expression on Symonton's face. She did not think it was appreciation for her insightful remarks about his character that she saw reflected in his expression.

"I was waiting to see if there were more of my secrets you wished to expose. How do you know all that?" Claire's words had left Symonton curiously shaken; she'd been so very certain in her analysis, so certain and so very accurate, besides.

"About you? An observant guess is all. I have little brothers, you know."

He took two broad steps to catch up with her and they began once more to stroll, Bonaparte following along behind.

"Now I think you have insulted as well as invaded."

"Not at all. I'm very fond of my brothers," and smiled as he threw back his head to laugh aloud.

"I see now what magic you wove to charm your Aunt Sophie out of her widow's weeds and transform that gray and mildewed monstrosity of a house into an elegant home."

"Does it seem like magic to you?" Claire asked thoughtfully after taking a moment to digest his comment. "It's nothing of the sort, you know. Just a lot of hard work and constantly biting one's tongue."

"Which gets tedious sometimes, I know." Symonton had heard the sound of a sigh in her voice, a touch of weariness, and more than a little frustration. For one quick moment he'd felt a spontaneous urge to offer her whatever she needed to make her life easier. She'd come such a long way with her three charges in tow, four if you counted Babu, and she was, after all, just one slender, hazel-eyed — he hadn't noticed until the sun touched her face just then that there were flecks of gold in her eyes — young woman.

"I can't imagine that you know, since I doubt you've had cause to bite your tongue all that often. I seem to recall being taken to task for something purely accidental and out of my control."

"Devil cat, you mean."

"Yes. Poor Babu. He and Cece both need lots of warmth and sunshine to be happy and both have suffered from heat deprivation since we arrived."

"Your sister is an astonishing beauty."

They came to an arrangement of large rocks tumbled together on the side of a hill, the result of some farmer's hard work when clearing his pastureland. Claire sank down on one flat boulder, Symonton on another opposite her.

"She is, isn't she? And so sweet-natured and intelligent, besides. Cece's a babu herself, though, and I need to be sure she has a secure life and a place where she is cherished and happy." At his inquiring look, she explained, "A *babu* is a term for someone neither Indian nor English, someone caught between cultures or between races. Cece's mother was from the most prestigious Indian aristocracy, from the family of the Rajah of Lahore in northwest India. My father married her after we'd been in India for about a year. I was seven years old and excited about having a new mother. I know Papa married for love, but practically speaking the marriage helped establish an alliance with her family, as well. Her dowry was an area rich in tea that my father had admired from his arrival in India. Tragically, Cece's mother died in childbirth and my sister was raised as an Englishwoman, although some of my—of our—countrymen have been disparaging in their treatment of her, so certain of their superior lineage without knowing one thing about my sister's heritage. Ignorance and prejudice are a deadly and insufferable combination."

Symonton heard the note of outrage, of iron, too, in her voice and imagined she could be the very devil if it came to protecting her sister.

"My nephew seems besotted with her and not disparaging at all," he responded and saw a crease appear between Claire's brows.

"Cece has that effect on young men, and I'm sure it will pass in Harry's case without any long-term damage. Cece hasn't come out yet, you know."

"I'd guess she's nearly twenty, though, isn't she, and able to make up her own mind? She's not really a school room miss at that age. I wouldn't know from my own experience, but I'm told that marriage and any love that might come with the institution are private and individual matters."

"Cece is a very young twenty," Claire retorted firmly, "and still needs guidance."

"From you, I presume." His tone was purposefully unreadable, but she thought she detected a slight scorn and it stung.

"I love her and want only what's best for her."

"And you don't think twenty is old enough to know one's own heart and mind?" Symonton knew he ought to let the subject drop but for some perverse reason was unable to do so; Claire Penwarren's confidence was a new kind of challenge for him. He continued with ruthless practicality, "I may, of course, be mistaken—though I admit to a certain deserved reputation for grasping the finer points of the female temperament—but your sister seems very self-possessed and mature for her age. Besides, she had you as an example, and when you were twenty were you not perfectly sure of what you wanted and what best suited you?"

"That was different," the words quick and slightly defensive.

"Ah," was Symonton's only rejoinder, but Claire met his eyes and gave a small, self-deprecating grimace in response.

"I sound managing and condescending, don't I? I don't mean to. Truly. I just want Cece to be happy, to make an advantageous marriage and have a secure and contented life."

"Do you plan to select this advantageous paragon of a husband for her?"

"Of course, not! I wouldn't dream of it!" Claire's tone was indignant. "But I may steer her in a certain direction. That's not so very managing, is it?"

"Let me guess. You are looking for wealth and a title."

There was something in Symonton's tone that told Claire the discussion of her sister's marital prospects had somehow shifted onto more sensitive ground, but she replied candidly, "I will not be so disingenuous as to try to convince you that I scorn wealth, but Cece will bring a comfortable dowry to her marriage, and she has some priceless jewels in her own name inherited from her mother, the value of which could support her for life. A title is impressive, I suppose, but hardly necessary for happiness. In fact, begging your pardon, I think it might just clutter Cece's life. All that who sits where and who gets introduced first and what's the proper title to use causes her undue anxiety, and the proprieties of the peerage can be so tiresome sometimes."

"I couldn't agree more," Symonton said, his clear blue eyes suddenly alight and the weary scorn in his voice gone. "Tiresome is exactly right. I've found it so for years. So if not wealth and a title, what are the requirements for your sister's model husband?"

"Someone who will be kind to her and will love her for more than her appearance," answered Claire promptly. She brought both feet up onto a flat shelf of the rock where she sat and wrapped her arms around her skirted knees as she spoke.

An undignified posture, Symonton thought, even as he appreciated that Claire was thinking through her answer with grave seriousness. No self-respecting woman, married or not, while in the company of one of England's most eligible peers would have arranged herself into so undignified a pose, but Claire seemed completely unheeding. He thought that small realignment of posture said something about how she regarded him, something not necessarily complimentary. Would she have been on more proper behavior if she felt any desire to impress him? The thought rankled.

"And someone of good character and good family," Claire continued, "who will protect her and put her happiness above his own. My sister is very precious to me, and if I can accomplish so happy a union I can go back to India satisfied and content."

His lordship raised his dark brows at that. He had been curious about the selfless pride he'd detected on Claire's face when all eyes had turned toward Cecelia that first visit to Loden Hall. Not many women enjoyed being outshone, even by a dearly loved sister.

"Your devotion to your sister is admirable," he commented in a dry tone, keeping even the slightest hint of curiosity out of his voice "Have you no plans for an advantageous marriage of your own?" Claire gave a little crow of laughter at the idea, a natural sound without self-consciousness or artifice.

"Oh, no! I'm fortunate to have my own income from my mother which allows me to remain independent without the fear of penury, and my father has spoiled me for marriage, besides. He's let me run the house from childhood, allowed me to establish the household budget and then put all the money I requested at my disposal, and entrusted every major domestic decision of our lives to my judgment. There's no husband that could endure my ways, and none that I could tolerate without braining him in short order. I will be perfectly happy managing my father's home, whether in India or England, and dandling my nieces and nephews on my knee. Our society has a long and noble tradition of the spinster aunt and I intend to do my part to uphold the custom. Once I get Cece safely married and my brothers situated with exactly the right tutor, I'll have accomplished the missions that brought me to England and can return to the happy task of caring for my father wherever that takes me."

Symonton had been so struck by Claire's words and even more disconcerted by the way the sun burnished her gleaming hair red-gold that he missed her next question and had to ask her, somewhat guiltily, to repeat it. Claire made a dismissive gesture and stood up, laughing as she shook out her skirts.

"I see I have begun to bore you and I beg your pardon for that. I'll need to improve my ability to recognize the signs of your dwindling interest. I simply asked if you knew of a suitable tutor for my brothers but don't answer now. I've already usurped too much of your morning." She picked up her walking stick, her words once more slightly shy, "But I did appreciate your audience. Sometimes it helps just to talk things through out loud, and I really haven't a friend to do that with here."

Symonton rose, too, and in a tone so free of selfishness or laziness it would have amazed anyone who knew him said, "Feel free to use me as a friend any time. I am at your disposal." He was as surprised as she at the offer.

"How kind of you! Thank you. I may do exactly that, but I promise not to abuse the privilege. I know you reached your limit with my chatter several minutes ago but were too kind to say anything."

"I cannot recall that I have ever been accused of being too kind and am at a loss for suitable words to respond." Symonton was himself again, cool and flippant.

"'I like your silence; it the more shows off your wonder,'" Claire quoted over her shoulder as she walked away, giving a little wave as she did so.

The Most Honourable Robert Septimus Louis Carlisle, Marquis of Symonton and Baron Carlisle of several lesser regions watched Claire Penwarren until she disappeared over a small hill, until he could no longer see even a shadow of her sturdy figure, and still he stood there, feeling as gauche as a schoolboy and conscious of some inner stirring that was entirely new to him. Not love, of course, since it bore no resemblance to what he'd felt for any of the beautiful women he'd kept under his protection through the years. No, this was something entirely different from those other, more easily recognized sensations he experienced when in the proximity of an attractive paramour. Symonton identified his swirl of emotion as a strong and single-minded desire to make life as easy as possible for Claire Penwarren, to carry her burdens when she allowed him to do so, to be a true friend and provide whatever service she needed, and to do it all with no expectation of thanks or reward. Altruism was as foreign to the man as Hindu prayer and just as mystifying. Behind him Bonaparte snorted and Symonton turned, brushed a hand across his brow as if clearing away cobwebs, and gathered up the reins.

"I was right, she does weave a spell," he said to the animal as he swung into the saddle, "but I find being bewitched has an appeal I never imagined."

For her part, Claire was only a trifle preoccupied with Symonton on her way home. The man had turned out to be much more companionable than she'd expected, that unbecoming air of arrogance and laziness he usually wore replaced by genuine interest, a defined and intelligent humor, and — most surprising of all — an unexpected but quite practical common sense. That would teach her to judge a book by its cover, she told herself firmly. Doing so was one of her prime character flaws and something she often promised herself she would rectify. Someday. Symonton would be good motivation for her to be less judgmental. She had initially thought that the combination of white-gold hair, cut too austerely short to be fashionable, and light, icy eyes made him unattractive and unapproachable, but she had revised her opinion the other afternoon as she observed him amusing the twins. Today her opinion had done another complete turnaround. His lordship had an inviting laugh, a way of listening that was flattering but not false, and the willingness to speak the truth, even when she did not particularly want to hear the truth.

That realization allowed her to review their discussion about Cecelia's future in a less reactionary manner. Symonton was right, after all. Eight years ago, when she had turned twenty, she had already been running her father's home for years and would have resented anyone telling her what future she ought to plan for herself or what kind of husband she ought to seek or even whether she ought to seek a husband at all. Of course, Cecelia at twenty was not the same as she had been at twenty, and Cece had an older sister to care for her and guide her, a luxury Claire herself never had. Their father traveled a great deal of the time and because both her stepmothers had died at shockingly young ages, Claire had first had to learn to take care of herself without a mother's guidance and then be sister and mother to three children in the house. She'd had no time to spend on being missish or bashful, no spare moments to seek out advice or ask opinions, even if there had been someone in the house to act as counselor.

Still, Claire had the nagging thought that there might be a kernel of truth to what Symonton had gently suggested. Marriage and the good fortune of love with marriage were private decisions, and Cecelia was twenty now, old enough to know her own mind and heart. Claire quieted her small sense of discomfort by assuring herself that she would never, could never, compel Cece to marry any particular man. Ultimately, the choice of a husband would be her sister's decision paired with her father's approval. Claire had no overt role in the process at all, but surely that did not mean she couldn't weigh in with her own opinion, which for all these years had done well for everyone in the family. Her father would be the first to credit Claire's uncommonly sound sense for his happy home so there was no reason she should feel guilty about taking some small responsibility for Cece's future. She had been making decisions about her family's future for years, and no one had complained about it yet.

Much to his family's surprise, Symonton continued to cool his heels at his sister's home well into April. If Margaret was curious about her brother's continued willingness to rusticate in the Sussex countryside, she wisely refrained from questioning him. His friends, awaiting his arrival in London for the beginning of the bustling social season, made certain ribald comments about country attractions and didn't give the matter additional thought. Symonton was a rule to himself, they agreed, always one to resist the ordinary and walk close to but never quite cross the line that would keep him from being acceptable in polite society. Of course, that line was different and much more flexible for him than for other gentlemen, possessed as he was with title, several estates, and an inheritance that had taken on mythical proportions. Every spring well-intentioned mamas invited him to meet their daughters newly hatched into the social world. Every spring Symonton made an appearance, dressing exactly right and saying all the right things, and with the constancy of the seasons themselves emerged from the experience unattached in status and unscathed in heart. In spite of his appearance for the mothers (bordering on the rakish, the elder women murmured uneasily, the contrast of those dark brows and that gleaming hair almost indecent) and because of his appearance for the daughters (definitely rakish, the younger women whispered hopefully, that lean face and those remarkable blue eyes incredibly attractive) Symonton had been a prime catch for the last decade. There had been that one disreputable incident years before, but memory was convenient when it came to eligible peers of the realm and no one chose to remember the details any longer. Some scandal or other, but young men of Symonton's background sowed their wild oats with the careless abandon of rabbits, and no one could recall the particulars any longer or even cared about them. In fact, the only person who had been affected by a youthful escapade that was now nothing more than an indistinct memory in the minds of middle-aged parents was Symonton himself. The affair, while healed over years before, had left behind a tough old scar from a wound he continued to feel.

Symonton, ever the strategist when it came to women, made it a point never to meet Claire on her morning walks more than twice a week and never on the same days of consecutive weeks. If he had been Harry's age, he would have ridden out every day and not given it a thought, as Harry, in fact, acted with Cecelia. Symonton enjoyed Claire's conversation and except for her would have been bored to distraction by the placid and uneventful country life which surrounded him. Her company on a daily basis would have mitigated the monotony, but he was older than Harry and with his years had come a certain cynical but practical wisdom. More than two meetings a week or joining her on the same two days of every week would have smacked of assignation and would have caused Claire misgivings. How he knew this he couldn't have explained, but he was as certain of Claire's reaction to any hint of over-familiarity on his part as he was of Harry's growing infatuation with Cecelia. Symonton was humbled by the realization that while he was fairly certain Claire enjoyed his company, was quick to understand and laugh at his comments, and sincerely appreciated his advice she did not consider him especially appealing or admirable. When he slipped into certain affected habits of speech or manner, he detected a veiled look in her eyes that told him without the need for any words that at that moment she found him, if not completely repellent, at least unattractive to the extreme. Such displeasure was a new experience for him, since for years his position and fortune had earned him almost infinite forgiveness and had allowed him to say or do almost anything without fear of social or personal chastisement. Claire, however, did not allow him that same license. On more than one occasion with her Symonton detected the same tone he'd heard on that first visit to Loden Hall when Matt had been excited about the fish pond story.

"I'm not sure what to make of the wager part," Claire had remarked casually but something about her, something untraceable but definite, had said she knew exactly what to make of foolish wagers and it was nothing complimentary. Symonton guessed Claire had learned to make her opinion known without words because of her brothers. Sometimes with boys—with grown men apparently, too—one could not come at things straight on. Sometimes a bland comment and a barely dampening tone were as effective, perhaps even more effective, than a scolding. On such occasions and without belaboring the point further, Claire would move casually on to another topic and leave the listener hastily reviewing the previous conversation in his mind to find where he'd offended. The tactic worked frequently and successfully with Symonton over the weeks, and he was hardly a boy, six and thirty on his last birthday and a wealth of experience with women in his past. Still, when that *something* crept into Claire's manner, he would find himself mentally searching through his recent words to discover what he might have said to cause the sparkle in her eyes and the lilt of laughter in her voice to diminish.

Symonton wouldn't have caused Claire any kind of discomfort for the world. In public settings, whether church— his sister was still recuperating from the shock of his request to join her at worship service—or a neighborhood gathering, the vicar's small dinner party or a light-hearted country dance hosted by the squire, Symonton was careful not to seek Claire out or even look in her direction more than once. Because he was who he was, people noticed such things even in the country, and he would not expose Claire to gossip or speculation. Such careful decorum was as new for him as attending regular worship. If he thought seriously about his behavior, and he usually tried not to do so, he told himself that he admired Claire Penwarren and did not want to jeopardize their friendship. No other woman had ever interacted with him as Claire did, her manner friendly and frank and no ulterior motives hiding in the depths of her fine hazel eyes. He found he liked that very much, that it was a relief not to have to look for secondary meanings hidden below the surface of her words. For Symonton, the art of flirtation had lost its appeal years ago. Now it was only a tedious and predictable necessity. Claire was direct and honest but never unkind, practical without losing her sense of humor and most especially her ability to laugh at herself. He liked all that very much and did whatever he must to maintain the limited time he could safely spend with her.

So twice a week on days that he hoped appeared random, he would walk with her and talk about the daily activities of her life, answer her questions and give his opinion when asked, make her laugh and accept her chastisement when he stepped over the line of good taste. The relationship suited him in its simplicity. He did not miss the new social season or the city or any of his friends. He was never bored in Claire's company and while he found Cecelia's placid good temper admirable but dreadfully tedious, the twins' high spirits added a certain piquancy to his days that made him actually enjoy the idea of spending extended time in their company. He envisioned inviting them on the kind of adventure boys their age would appreciate—although except for fishing he hadn't any idea what kind of adventure that would be, and try as he might he really could not picture himself lounging on a river bank with a fishing pole in one hand and an old meerschaum pipe in the other. Still, Symonton found the novelty of contentment so satisfying that he began to contemplate moving in with his sister on a permanent basis in order that life could continue exactly as it was for years to come.

That was why, when Claire told him that all the Penwarrens were going to London for several weeks, his immediate reaction was to protest.

"You've hardly had a chance to settle in here," Symonton said, unable to keep a rather unattractive whining tone from creeping into his words. Claire heard the whine, too, and chose to ignore it. She had learned early on that Symonton did not like his routine, even something as innocent as an early morning stroll, upset. Everything must be on his terms. It was how he was put together.

The month of April spread its glories all around them as they walked, Lent and Easter well past and everything blossoming and bursting with intemperate license. This particular morning was sun-kissed, the sky cloudless and blue, wildflowers poking white and yellow and purple through the grass. Claire and Symonton, walking side-by-side like two old and comfortable friends who'd known each other for years instead of months, ended up at the gathering of rocks they had used on their first meeting. It had become their drawing room of sorts.

"Why would you give up a Sussex spring for the fleshpots of London?" Symonton demanded, looming over Claire like a colossus.

"My point exactly, Symonton, and do sit down, will you? When you hover in such an intimidating manner I begin to suspect a lecture and I warn you, I am in no mood to be lectured about anything. You of all people must realize that there simply aren't enough fleshpots in the neighborhood." Claire sat down and spread her skirts primly around her before pulling off the kerchief she wore over her hair to wipe a smudge of something from the back of her hand.

For just a moment Symonton was distracted by the auburn red of her hair. Claire was always the soul of propriety, not an inch of unnecessary skin showing and her hair always under a hat or scarf so that he almost forgot how it flamed to life in the sunshine.

"Symonton?" He forced his attention back to the conversation at hand as Claire continued with a laugh, "Have I lost you already? Oh, dear, I must truly be failing in my ability to conduct lively conversation. I count on you to keep me practiced so if my conversation is less than entertaining, the deficiency is your fault."

He followed her orders and sat, too, directly across from her so he could watch the play of early morning light on Claire's skin.

"I wouldn't get too smug, my dear. I daresay I drift off much more often than you realize."

Claire shook her head, no longer giving the *my dear* a second thought. The tone Symonton used held no presumption of endearment or intimacy other than that of an older, wiser, world-weary brother.

"I doubt that. You're never very good at hiding your feelings when you find something to be dreary or dull. I thought you were going to explode in the vicar's front parlor Saturday evening."

"Is that why you burst so suddenly into that outlandish story about elephants?" She chuckled.

"Was it so obvious? I saw the look in your eyes and wanted to spare the vicar and his wife from whatever biting comment trembled on your tongue."

"What a self-absorbed creature you must think me!" Claire looked at him quickly and saw that he was not smiling.

"Please forgive me if I've offended you. I didn't mean it quite the way it sounded. The Waterstons are dear and decent people, but I doubt those are qualities you find tolerable over an extended evening, and even Aunt Sophie found it difficult to maintain an interest in vegetable marrows. I daresay we should all have benefited from hearing the vicar quote from Carouthers' sermons at the slightest provocation, and the dear man did it with the best of intentions, but if I felt restive I knew it had to be much worse for you. I didn't mean to sound patronizing just now, and I don't think you're self-absorbed— well, not so very often, anyway." Symonton tried not to wince at the unconscious prick of her words. Claire was not a woman to spare his feelings. "I know you enjoy giving the impression that you're self-absorbed, but I also know that you can be very kind—you have been to me, anyway—and I was trying to return the favor."

She was sincere in her contrition, which Symonton wished she hadn't felt obligated to voice. He *was* self-absorbed and everyone who knew him accepted it. He had agreed to dinner at the vicarage only because he knew Claire would be there, so he had gone for his own pleasure, as self-serving as everyone imagined and undeserving of any apology.

"Never mind. Tell me about London instead."

"Ah, London. Well, part of the reason we're going is very practical. I must find a man who will do as a tutor for both Will and Matt. They really need two separate instructors, of course, all the sciences and the mysteries of mechanics for Will, and I'm not sure what exactly for Matt." She sighed. "The basics to start with, I'm afraid, because if the topic is not connected in some way with horseflesh or pugilism, Matt is totally disinterested. He's not much of a scholar."

"Does that trouble you?" asked Symonton. He had come to recognize the expressions of her face: joy, kindness, sympathy and mischief, worry and concern and infrequent pique. What he saw just then was definitely concern.

"Matt is the heir and a lot will be expected of him in that role. He has so much to learn, but a love of horses and fighting aren't really primary traits for responsible living. They sound too much like my Uncle Thomas, and it hasn't taken me long to get his measure, even if it is posthumous. I fear I wouldn't have enjoyed his company very much." Symonton, who had known Thomas Penwarren, nodded his agreement.

"Matt's just a boy, Claire." He had slipped easily into her first name in their private conversations but was careful to use proper address in public company. "He'll settle down."

She smiled a thank you to him for his encouraging words, but he could tell she still felt doubts about Matt's future.

"So you go to London seeking two paragons, then?" Symonton asked. She laughed, not needing to ask for an explanation, which for Symonton was one of her most sterling qualities. There was nothing slow about Claire Penwarren.

"Exactly. One for my brothers and one for Cecelia. Your Harry's attentions are becoming a little too pointed and constant for my comfort, and I want Cece to have the opportunity to meet other young men."

"Shall I tell Harry to stay home?" Claire saw that he was serious and felt a small pang on Harry's behalf.

"No, thank you. That would be too unkind to both of them. I think if I simply take Cece away for a few weeks, their attraction will die a natural death. He's a nice enough young man, Symonton, so I hope I am not offensive, only I can't think Cece would enjoy the lot of a soldier's wife, the travel and lengthy separations, so much responsibility in his absence and always the general fear for his safety, besides. I want something more stable for her."

"What does Cecelia say about all this?" Symonton used the tone of gentle rebuke Claire had come to dislike, the tone that made her feel both guilty and cranky.

"Cece is very biddable and has been all her life. She's quiet and attentive and I believe—I know—she trusts my judgment."

"But what does she say about your plans for London?" he pressed and Claire's face flushed.

"She is less than excited, as you may well have guessed." At his continued wordless gaze she added defensively, "She simply doesn't understand. How could she? She's never experienced a season. Once she sees her beautiful new gowns, attends dances and parties and the theater, meets new gentlemen friends and makes new friends in general, she'll thank me."

"Your sister doesn't strike me as a young woman for whom any of those heady temptations would hold much attraction." In one of her rare tempers, Claire stood up abruptly.

"I know her better than you, Symonton, and I love her, besides. When we're in London, Cece will enjoy herself and do all the things young women should have the opportunity to do."

He still sat, eyeing her calmly. "Did you have those opportunities?"

"No, of course not. It's not as if we were in Calcutta or Delhi where there was a strong English presence and some semblance of an English society. We were up in the northern hills, and I told you I was too busy with the household for those kinds of fripperies."

"And you still seem to have a happy life." The irony of his arguing against indulgence and expensive pastimes was lost on her.

"Really, Symonton," Claire said crossly, "I'm an old maid. Our family can support one but not two of us, and it's hardly the life I'd wish for my sister, anyway. Cece is too sensitive to enjoy lifelong solitude." She covered that glorious hair with a yank of the scarf. "We leave for London on Friday and we will have a delightful time." She stamped one foot for emphasis before the ridiculousness of her words and her own bad temper struck her sense of humor and made her laugh aloud, her good nature restored. "So there," she concluded. She looked at him with a smile. "I do appreciate that I don't have to bite my tongue with you or always flutter around with apologies when I'm cross. I'll miss that when we're gone."

"As it turns out, I plan to leave for London as well," Symonton rejoined, making the information up on the spot. "My sister has been secretly hoping for my departure for weeks now, and I find it harder and harder to bear up under her urgent disapproval."

"You say the most outrageous things! Coming out of Easter vespers, Lady Pasturson told me how delighted she was to have you with her for an extended visit this season."

"My sister is very well bred. She would hardly admit to you that she had my empty bags placed in the hallway outside my door several days ago as a broad hint of her wishes." Claire gave a gurgle of laughter.

"What a goose you are, Symon!" Without prompting, she had naturally and unaffectedly adopted the name only his closest intimates were invited and permitted to use. He would have reproved the liberty in anyone else, but he enjoyed hearing her use the name. "Perhaps that means we'll see you in London, then. We've rented a house and Aunt Sophie is coming with us to lend proper countenance. I can't imagine we will enjoy any of the same activities or frequent the same habitats as you, but if you see us, please promise not to cut us with your usual icy edge."

"Do I have an icy edge?"

"Oh, my, yes. Sometimes I'm quite chilled. Harry tells us that in some circles you're known as the Ice Man, so I must assume others have felt your frigid blast, as well."

"Harry has a youthful indiscretion about him that I hope the military will be able to control. Clearly I have not been successful in doing so."

"Don't be angry with him. I think one of the boys was pumping him for information about you and the words just popped out."

"I hope he didn't share anything more damaging."

"Not in mixed company, Symonton, and not in front of children. Even in the deepest throes of infatuation, Harry knows better than to do that." Claire laughed over at him, slim and a little more sun-browned than was fashionable. "So will we see you in London, do you think?"

He stood. "It could happen, I suppose, but I might be at the stage door of the theater instead of in the seats. You and I would be interested in different performances." She laughed again, accustomed by now to his outrageous pronouncements.

"Don't try to shock me with your scandalous lifestyle. I have no doubt you've made the acquaintance of every beautiful actress in London."

"Making their acquaintance isn't exactly how I would phrase it, but I can't argue with the thought." Claire gave a little twist of her mouth as she stood.

"There's always a certain appeal to a rake, isn't there? I've never understood it myself. Well, we like you anyway and as long as you're not dangling after Cecelia, you may be as profligate and prodigal as you choose."

"Thank you. Your permission relieves my troubled conscience." She ignored his comment and raised her hand in a small gesture of farewell.

"We won't see you for a while, Symonton. Please do take care of yourself. Your sister said you usually come to the Valley for Christmas so if not sooner, I hope we see you then."

Later, cantering on Bonaparte all the way home, Symonton sent Claire a mental promise: You will see me much sooner than Christmas, my dear. Of that you may be absolutely certain.

Chapter 5

When Claire first suggested the trip to London, Cecelia had for the first time in Claire's memory resisted her sister's plans and had done so with a gentle single-mindedness that would not be dissuaded.

"But I like it here now," Cece said, her mouth firmly set. She had never incurred Claire's anger—just the thought of it was enough to turn her stomach upside down—but she could not help her response. "Must we go somewhere new again, Claire? It was such a long trip to Sussex and it has been only a few weeks since we arrived. Why can't we just settle in for a while and enjoy Loden Hall?"

Claire had patiently explained that London emptied for the summer and if they were to enjoy any part of the social season, they must go now. "We'll be back in a few weeks," Claire pointed out, "and the time will fly. You'll see. If nothing else, think of poor Aunt Sophie. She's been in mourning for a year and even before that she hardly ever got out. Would you deprive her of the chance to renew old acquaintances?"

"Why don't you and she go then? I could stay here and be perfectly happy." Cecelia could not bring herself to let the matter go. In the past she had acquiesced to every idea of her elder sister, but she had other emotions now besides sisterly devotion, although it would not do to share any of those feelings with Claire. The idea of doing so made Cecelia even more queasy.

I'm sure you'd be overjoyed to stay behind, thought Claire, especially if one particular, handsome, nicely-mannered young neighbor were staying behind, too. Well, that affair needed to be nipped and to Claire's mind, a trip to London would do exactly that. Harry Macapee was a fine young man, but he was still the only eligible young man Cecelia had met since their arrival in Sussex. Claire felt quite certain that once her sister met other young men, she would recognize Harry's deficiencies and thank Claire for carrying her off Sabine-style to London. For just a moment Claire felt quite ashamed of herself. All that made

Harry Macapee unsuitable in her eyes was a certain lack of social stability, and she knew that was not truly a deficiency, at least not the kind that mattered when it came to the character of one's family and friends. Her own father had been a second son, and he was successful in all areas of his life—family, friends, and finances—and by all accounts was an all around better man than his established older brother had ever been. Claire made herself banish any further thoughts on the topic and soothed her discomfort with the thought that she was thinking only of Cecelia.

In the end, Claire got her way as she always did, but Cece's tragic dark eyes and drawn face threatened to spoil the fun of the visit.

"She'll get over it when she attends her first ball," said Sophie to Claire. "Ain't a gal alive who can resist the music and the chatter. You'll see. You may find that even someone of your advanced years will enjoy herself." Sophie had become fond of Claire, seeing a little of herself in her niece's strong will and common sense.

"I love to dance," admitted Claire, "but there was little enough opportunity for it where we were. A few times a year Papa took us to Delhi for shopping and to meet with friends so there were dances and parties then, but other than that it was Cece and I gliding around the front lawn humming a melody and pretending we were princesses. For Cece that was almost true, but if ever there were a woman not a princess, it was I."

"Your father didn't do you any service keeping you hidden away in that heathen land. You don't have the looks of your sister, that's true, but you're still a handsome girl with pretty manners and good blood. You could have had a family of your own by now if Philip had done the right thing by you."

Claire would not hear her father criticized and replied tersely, "I would not have had it any other way, Aunt. With only distant relations left on my mother's side, where would I have gone?"

"You could have come to his lordship and me. I know I asked Philip to send you here often enough, but he wouldn't hear of losing you. I'd have enjoyed the company of a daughter in the house."

Claire heard the unspoken loneliness and regret in her aunt's voice and didn't speak further on the subject. Her father didn't need her defense, anyway. He had frequently offered to send her to family in England, but she was the one who wouldn't hear of it. She had missed out on some things, she supposed, but she had gained much more than she had lost. No one could have separated her from Papa and her sister and brothers. The idea of being sent away from them at any time in the last two decades had been too dreadful to contemplate.

"It's too late now, Aunt, to think about the past, and we're not going to London so I can find a dancing partner, though I intend to enjoy myself. It's Cecelia who's the true attraction and the reason for the trip. I'm relieved you can come with us. Even at my years, there might have been a hint of impropriety if I set up housekeeping on my own."

Sophie snorted. "Your years, indeed! As if eight and twenty was Methuselah."

"Alas, I am no longer a sweet flower of youth," laughed Claire, "and I can't tell you what a relief that is! Cece will have two chaperones so no possible taint of unseemliness will attach to her. We will all have a good time, and I can't wait to show off my sweet sister to London society. She'll cause a stir no one will soon forget."

In that respect, Claire was correct. They traveled comfortably to London to a spacious and classic house on Millefore Square, Sophie, Claire, Cecelia, and Babu in one coach, the boys, Crayton, Moira, and Feastwell in another. Mrs. Feastwell was so excited at the prospect she stammered her words when Claire first presented the idea of the staff accompanying the family to London, and Crayton, who had slowly come around to the idea that doing real work wasn't all that bad when it was appreciated and rewarded, was for the first time in memory speechless. Both women had endured the parsimony of the old lord and never expected the adventure of a stay in the city. Moira, filled out into a pretty girl and dressed as a proper lady's maid, kept very still. It was all more than she had ever expected in her young life, and she was afraid someone would realize they'd made an awful mistake and send her back to the dark, crowded cottage where the remaining eleven members of her family lived. The three servants had bonded in an unspoken but forceful way, united with one common goal: the protection of their family. Nothing in the house should be allowed to give anyone, especially Miss Claire, one little moment of disquiet. They recalled what it had been like under old Lord Loden and not a day passed when they didn't count their blessings and send up a wordless but grateful prayer to whatever divinity had sent them these specific Penwarrens.

Upon arrival, Feastwell made the London kitchen hers in a matter of minutes, kindly cowed the scullery maid who came with the house, and within the space of twenty-four hours knew where to shop for the freshest greens and the most tender meat. Crayton clucked with dismay at the cloths over the furniture, the dust on the picture frames, and the one noticeable threadbare patch on the carpet in the morning room.

She had Betcher help her move a heavy walnut sideboard over the worn spot and would not be quiet about it until Betcher finally said, "Enough carping, Crayton. It ain't like guests will see the morning room. That's only family, after all."

To which Crayton, drawing herself up to ramrod rigidity, responded with dignity, "It's the family that matters and should have the best. I'm not concerned about a motley group of strangers that have the good fortune to make the acquaintance of our ladies. They should count themselves privileged to be in the same room with them, let alone make any critical comment about the furnishings."

Upstairs Moira was helping Cecelia unpack, awed by the dresses she was hanging, admiring all the colors and fabrics, the silks stitched with gold and pretty flowered muslins, satins in rich colors of ruby and emerald and in softer hues of peach and cream.

"Oh, Miss," said the girl, "ain't they beautiful?"

Cecelia, seeing Moira's glowing face, hadn't the heart to say what she felt, that none of it mattered to her, not the dresses or the hats, the kid gloves or silk stockings or shiny, square-toed shoes Claire had purchased for her in abundance.

"Yes, they are, Moira, very beautiful. Such pretty colors. Do you have a favorite color?" Like Claire, Cecelia had a kind heart and a soft spot for the very young or vulnerable.

"Oh, green, Miss. I love green."

Cecelia, thinking of the Sussex countryside flourishing in spring greens and the young man she'd left behind there, sighed. "Yes, green is my favorite color, too."

Moira saw the sadness on Cece's striking face and felt as if she wanted to do battle with whatever caused that look. Someone as beautiful as Miss Cecelia should always be happy; her smile had the ability to make everyone else feel happy, too.

Later, downstairs in the kitchen, Moira asked Crayton, "Why do you think Miss Cecelia looks so sad?" and Crayton, not one to gossip with the lower orders, only said, "Love and money, missy, are the only two things that cause real grief, and Miss Cecelia has money to burn," leaving Moira to figure it out on her own.

More than once in the first week there, Claire had cause to thank her Aunt Sophie. The older woman's presence opened doors that otherwise might have been closed to them. Old acquaintances and girlhood friends heard that Sophie Penwarren was in town—surely the first time since her coming out over thirty years ago—and came knocking on the front door in quantity. Calling cards filled the hallway and invitations soon followed.

Besides her wide network of acquaintances, Sophie also had a memory for gossip and a clear, objective eye for screening and selecting invitations.

"I was in the Sussex countryside, not banished to Russia," she explained to Claire, "and I had my ways of keeping in touch with the latest *ondits*. You can trust me to know which ones are wrong'ns. Now this invitation is pretty enough"—she held up the pink envelope with its sprig of dainty flowers engraved in the corner for Claire to view—"but send your regrets. Fine paper don't make up for the fact that the Ballantines have always been common as pond water. The Fitzhughs are another story. No daughters and two eligible sons if I recall. The Gibbons' musical evening will be a dead bore but anyone who's anyone will be there and so will we. Wear something missish Thursday evening; the duke has a sentimental regard for girls in pink, more's the pity for his wife." And so it went, Claire scrupulously following her aunt's direction on behalf of Cecelia, and Cecelia trying her best to be the perfect sister on behalf of Claire.

It didn't take long for reports about the newly-arrived Penwarren sisters to float through town. One or two afternoon calls, a well-bred word about two charming young women of good family with, so rumor had it, respectable fortunes and success was almost guaranteed.

Their first official ball was everything Claire had hoped for and more. She had never experienced such a crush of people, all of them strangers, and yet a devout silence seemed to precede and follow Cecelia wherever she went. Her warm, brunette beauty made all the other young women look as if they were recently recovering from serious illnesses. Cecelia wore pale raspberry taffeta, modestly off the shoulder with sleeves that began a dramatic flair midway down her arm.

"I can hardly raise my arms," she had protested and Claire, fussing with her sister's toilette, had responded practically, "You're not going to be climbing trees, Cece. You only need to be able to raise your arms enough to dance." Everything complete, Claire stepped back from her sister, clapping her hands softly in delight and then came to press a cheek against Cecelia's.

"You look stunning, my dear. I remember your mother looking just like you look this evening. She was beautiful, too, like you. Oh, I wish Papa could see you right now. He would be so proud of you!"

"Would he really?" Cecelia asked distinctly, her expression sober, and then not wanting to spoil Claire's evening, she smiled her brilliant smile to soften the quiet, ambiguous question. "You won't have time to worry about me this evening, Claire. You'll be too busy with your own admirers."

"Oh, pooh. I'll be sitting in the chaperone corner drinking lemonade." But Cecelia was right. In her own way Claire looked as striking as her sister, her hair parted down the middle and caught at the back of her neck and wearing a gown of sea green silk threaded through with gold and a gold shawl across her milky shoulders.

Aunt Sophie proclaimed that their debut would be bound to turn heads and cause comment and she was right. Claire, seeing Cecelia's dance card fill up, following her sister's graceful carriage, watching her gentle smile punctuate her conversation with just the right amount of modesty, entirely missed the fact that she was drawing as much attention as Cecelia. She was caught off guard by the line of hopeful dance partners but quickly recovered and laughed off the requests saying, "How kind of you, but I really must keep my Aunt Sophie company." Claire threaded her way through the crowd to the corner where her aunt sat.

"Make room for me," she whispered. "I'm being pursued." It was true. A portly man with an ill-proportioned mustache was close on her heels.

"Lady Claire?" Claire's stout pursuer stopped in front of her.

"Yes?" She looked up at him from her seat with what she hoped was courteous but detached interest. He was not someone to whom she had been introduced earlier, and there was some indefinable quality about the man that made Claire desire to keep it that way.

"How do you do? I'm Walter Thatcher. I hope you don't find me presumptuous, but I believe we're cousins and I wished to pay my regards." Claire found it awkward to sit and peer up at him so she stood to give him a closer look.

"I don't recall any Thatchers in the family, sir."

"My grandmother was Florence Goodwood before her marriage, and she and your mother's mother were sisters."

The names stirred a vague memory, and from behind Claire, Sophie said, "You're Florence Goodwood's grandson? Her daughter married a Thatcher as I recall. It's a baronetcy, ain't it, somewhere in Kent?" Thatcher turned his attention to Sophie.

"Yes, Lady Loden. My mother was Rosetta Stemberton, daughter of Florence Goodwood and Sir Albert Stemberton, and my father was Sir Montague Thatcher. They're all gone now and I have little enough family so I was pleased to hear of Lady Claire's arrival in England." He held out his hand for Claire's dance card. "I hope you've saved at least one dance for me, cousin."

Claire thought the "cousin" overfamiliar for an initial meeting but also apparently true if Sophie was to be believed, and she gave in graciously.

"I have this one free, Sir Walter, if that suits," and without delay found herself dancing her first dance of the evening with a long lost family member she wasn't sure she wanted and knew she didn't need. She was in danger of leaping to one of her usual conclusions about the fellow based on the flow of his conversation whenever they were joined together by the dance, a conversation punctuated too often with the word *I*. Then there was the way he had at first officiously fitted her hand under his arm as if she needed avuncular guidance to locate the dance floor and he was just the man to do it. Claire disliked being herded or patronized and she feared her cousin—distant, but alas, not distant enough—was doing both. Still, he was family and so she remained pleasantly attentive and properly admiring. He appeared to need her to be both and Claire was grimly determined to oblige.

As they walked back together, Thatcher asked, "Where are you staying in London?" and Claire knew as soon as she gave the address that they would see him the next day.

Through the crowd she saw Cecelia and said, pride displayed in each word, "You must meet my sister, Cecelia."

Thatcher turned, gave Cece a brief, dismissive glance, and said to Claire, "Someone told me that was your sister, but I thought they must be mistaken. No Goodwood blood there, I'd wager," and gave a smug laugh that was offensive enough to darken the color of Claire's eyes and cause a warmth to creep up her cheeks.

She took a deep breath before stating calmly, "Thank you, Sir Walter, for refreshing my family memory. I find I am a trifle faint from the crush of people and require a seat immediately. No, please don't feel an obligation to accompany me," and without giving him a chance to respond she walked rapidly toward the side of the room where her aunt sat, leaving her cousin staring after her from the edge of the dance floor.

Claire recognized that she was angry enough to be indiscreet and that would never do. She needed a place to calm her temper and supposed some shadowy sideline would be exactly right. She had heard that same self-assured, disparaging tone from others who felt that any lineage not able to claim full and undiluted English blood all the way back to Adam and Eve was unacceptable and vulgar.

The pompous ass, Claire fumed inwardly, as if he were worth one of Cecelia's little fingers, and promptly bumped headlong into a large figure. Raising her gaze, she changed her hasty apology into a happy greeting.

"Symonton, where did you come from? I've been here all evening and didn't see you come in." He looked resplendent, all crisp black and white except for his startling blue eyes, wearing a perfect cravat with two small diamond studs, not a hair out of place or a wrinkle where it shouldn't be.

"I came in when you were dancing with the man whose murder you now contemplate."

"Oh, dear, is it that obvious? I thought I was looking quite placid."

"You look like you want to throttle him with your bare hands and then shake the life out of him for good measure. I felt I should step in to keep you from homicide. It's not the way to impress in your first season, you know."

"Oh, bother," said Claire. "I'll need to give more attention to maintaining a blasé and casual countenance under provocation. It is not, I fear, a character strength on my part. I am ashamed to say the man is a distant cousin on my mother's side who is relieved that Cecelia isn't in *his* family, tainted as she clearly is with non-English blood."

"He never said that," Symonton protested but thought from the bright color in Claire's cheeks that the fool must have said something very similar to put her in such high dudgeon.

"Not in so many words, and I think that somehow made it even worse. I feel like he shared some particularly nasty secret with me. But I don't want to talk about him any more. Did you see Cece? Oh, Symon, you should have been here when she arrived. The whole room went dumb with admiration when she entered, and she was so oblivious to it all, really so modest and kind. It was wonderful."

He said nothing but put a hand under her elbow and moved her along to the corner where Sophie sat. Somehow, Claire thought, being herded by Symonton wasn't objectionable at all, nothing like her cousin's officious care.

"So you decided to make an appearance, Symonton?" asked Sophie. "I wondered if we'd see you. I heard Margaret is coming up to town."

"Yes, she'll arrive next week and spend time with my niece, who's breeding. I expect Margaret will stay a few weeks.

Harry came up to town with me." Claire filed that little fact away, not pleased to hear it. Harry's presence could complicate matters.

"I wouldn't have thought this was quite your scene," Sophie said with a touch of malice. "Too many girls just out of the schoolroom. Not your type at all." Symonton looked around at the milling crowds.

"Every once in a while I spy a diamond amid all those milky pearls, Lady Loden, and it makes the evening worthwhile."

Sophie chuckled. "Speaking of diamonds, won't you take Claire onto the floor? She insists on burying herself with us ancients, but I consider it a waste."

He raised an eyebrow at Claire. "Have you an open space?"

"I have an abundance of open spaces because I was determined to chaperone with modest circumspection and sit out the evening on the sidelines. I would have, too, if I hadn't been ambushed by my obnoxious cousin."

He held out an arm. "Then at the risk of another ambush, may I?"

Symonton knew that he could dance only once with Claire if he did not want to cause any kind of speculative talk, and it would be even safer if he followed up by dancing once with Cecelia, too. No one would find it remarkable then. Country neighbors, they'd say, whose acquaintance he made when he visited his sister. All perfectly correct and understandable. If he could do what he wished—and he was used to doing just that— he would dance with Claire all evening, every dance, and when not dancing, he'd just sit across from her and watch her face, watch the rosy tint of color creep up her cheeks as she spoke, watch the way her eyes reflected the gold sparkle from the shawl she wore. Symonton had never seen Claire like this, all smooth shoulders and creamy skin, the swell of breast above the low neckline hinting at even more delight. He had looked for and found her immediately upon arrival, her anticipated presence the only reason he'd come in the first place, and from first sight she had stolen his breath away. Literally. He'd given a soft gasp and feared that for one very brief moment he had gaped at her like an awe-struck schoolboy. No walking stick and kerchief and muddied boots now. Claire Penwarren had turned into some other creature as surely as if she'd sprouted wings, a sumptuous and enticing creature lush with promise.

He had stepped back for a moment to regain his usual insouciance before traversing the room, careful to greet acquaintances and say all the right things, to scan the crowd with casual attention and not let his eyes linger on Claire for an inordinate length of time. Long and often enough, though, to spy her in someone else's arms.

Symonton, a man renowned for his cool languor, startled himself by having to restrain a violent urge to walk up to that man, whoever he was, and dunk his head in the punch bowl just on general principles. He had been concerned—but more relieved—to see temper flare in Claire's face, a face he had come to know astonishingly well in so short a time, as she turned abruptly and left her partner standing at the edge of the dance floor clearly surprised by her hasty departure. The man had said or done something to irk Claire, and Symonton was delighted that she had not bothered to cover her displeasure with the polite intricacies of acceptable public behavior. He knew her to be as adept at social interaction as he so the man must have really overstepped to send Claire storming away in such a precipitous fashion. Symonton thought she'd handled the situation exactly right but for reasons that would never have crossed Claire's mind. From his first sight of her that evening, it was obvious to Symonton, transparently and ridiculously obvious, that Claire Penwarren should not be in anyone's arms but his, and he was gratified that providence apparently agreed with him.

All this unusual emotion roiling around in the depths of Symonton's mind and heart did not surface in his words or tone or expression. Instead, once they had taken their place in the set, he had time to ask only "Have you uncovered Cecelia's paragon yet?" before they separated.

When they joined up again to promenade hand in hand with the other couples, Claire protested as if there had been no interruption following his question. "This is our first formal outing, and I've hardly had a chance to meet anyone. I have a plan, though."

"I thought you might."

"I'll casually quiz Cece each morning to see if there's anyone that struck her fancy and if I detect even the slightest interest on her part, I'll review his name and family with Aunt Sophie. You wouldn't believe it, Symonton, but Aunt Sophie seems to know everyone! Then when the gentleman in question calls, and I'm sure after this evening we'll have all sorts of young men at our door, I'll have a chance to observe him more closely and in a more informal setting. There it is: Cece, Sophie, me. If he passes all our inspections, he may be the man."

"Are you prepared to be disappointed if Cecelia doesn't show an interest in anyone?" Symonton asked gently.

Claire started to respond, but the music picked up and they had to separate again so the moment was lost. He thought she looked thoughtful and sober for a long minute, however, and supposed she was giving his question serious contemplation. He would be sorry if she were disappointed but considered that could very likely happen. Claire's cheerful belief that she could organize everyone's life was part of her charm, but he knew it might cause her future heartache. He cared little enough for most people and seldom gave a thought to the feelings of those around him, but even he, as purposefully oblivious to others' sensitivities as he was, realized that people were not playing pieces to be pushed about on a chess board. There was a perversity to human nature that sometimes made it resent being ordered about, even if it was for its own good. He himself was proof of that, having resisted any and all advice, no matter how wise, with youthful energy, even when he knew he was headed in the wrong direction. Claire had the best and most loving of intentions, but unless he was very much mistaken she was going to be disappointed in her aspirations for Cecelia and the failure would rankle, if not hurt. Symonton would have prevented any hurt from touching Claire if he could but feared it was already too late for that.

Once Symonton met his private obligation to claim Cecelia for one of the simpler country dances, he departed the party. Claire and Cecelia stayed on until Sophie declared they would risk being branded unfashionable if they waited too long to call for their wraps.

"Never be among the last crowd to leave," she told her nieces. "It makes you look desperate, and that's not the way you want others to see you," which made Claire decide that one of the wisest things she had ever done in her entire life was ask her Aunt Sophie to stay on with them. The woman was worth her weight in diamonds.

Cecelia was more than usually quiet on the trip home and Claire, dressed for bed, stopped in Cecelia's room before retiring. It was just possible that the first stage of her plan was moving forward and Cece was already mooning over someone she'd met that evening. Not that anything ever moved that quickly or smoothly, Claire told herself with a weary sigh, but it didn't hurt to hope.

"Did you enjoy yourself tonight, Cece?" she asked, coming into the room to sit on the edge of her sister's bed. Babu, stretched out against Cecelia's feet, showed his disapproval known by raising his steady, quiet purr briefly to a throaty growl, then curled into an even tighter ball and went back to sleep, satisfied he had made his opinion about late night disturbances perfectly clear.

Cecelia turned on her side to face Claire and propped her head up on one hand.

"Everything was very beautiful, the ladies in their colorful gowns and all the flowers, and I liked the music. People seemed kind, too."

"Why shouldn't they be kind? You were the most beautiful girl there, and everyone wanted to meet you. Who was that fair-haired young man I saw bringing you lemonade? He danced with you twice, didn't he? I think Aunt Sophie was getting ready to come over and drag you away from him. Three dances would have been remarked upon."

"He was The Honourable Charles Hustisford."

"So that was Viscount Steppington's son. I think Charles is the eldest, isn't he?" Cecelia gave no answer, only a slight shrug, but Claire persevered. "I thought him very handsome, Cece, and he seemed quite taken with you. Did you like him?"

Cecelia looked at her sister so long and so soberly that Claire was almost embarrassed at her shameless prying, but then Cece smiled and said, "I love you, Claire. You are the best sister anyone could have and I would talk to you all night if I were able, but I'm tired. Could we chat tomorrow instead?" She turned onto her back and pulled the covers up to her chin, causing an annoyed cat squeak from the foot of the bed.

"Of course."

Claire stood, blew out the lamp by the bed, and looked over at her sister, thick lashes against her cheeks and black hair a soft cloud against the pillow.

"I love you, too, Cece," Claire said softly, "and I only want you to be happy."

But Cecelia was already asleep and didn't hear her.

Chapter 6

$\mathcal{D}$espite the late night, Claire kept to her usual morning routine. She always waited for her brothers to rise and the three would take a walk to the local park before breakfast was set.

"Betcher says there's something called a diorama show," Matt told Claire eagerly the morning after the ball, "that's great fun. He said he'd take us, Claire. Please say we can go. Please."

"Since I have no idea what a diorama is, let me talk to Betcher first. Has either of you taken the time to do any lessons this week?" She knew a pang of guilt at the simultaneous shaking of their heads. "I think I'll talk to Symonton about a tutor for you, then. He might know of someone now that he's in town. Papa will be here before we realize it and your education will still be inadequate."

"I don't see why I have to know anything more than I already do," said Matt in a sullen tone. "When I'm grown, I'll have servants and a secretary to write letters and such. I can ask Betcher about the horses. I think all this attention to a tutor is a bother. It's all right for Will, his head is always stuck in a book, but I don't see why I should have to have any more learning."

This outburst surprised and alarmed Claire. She knew that over the past weeks she had focused on Cecelia and not spent much time with the boys, but after the long confinement of the trip, she had wanted to give them a chance just to be boys for a while. She'd had the work on the house and the grounds to supervise interspersed with an increasing number of visiting neighbors, and then she had to plan for the London trip. Everything had conspired to cause her to postpone finding a tutor, but hearing Matt's petulant tone made her realize she couldn't wait any longer. He was getting to an age where discipline and education were essential, and she did him no favor by neglecting the task.

"What of you, Will?" Claire asked, purposefully ignoring Matt for the time being.

Will was more subdued in his answer. "I want to know more, and if a tutor will do that for me, I wish you would get one. How will I be prepared for exploring Africa or America if I don't have the proper education?"

Claire digested all this information quietly as the three strolled on until she finally said, "Matt, I know you don't understand this, but Papa has always said that education makes the man, that there are things every man should know that can only be found in books. It's not intended to be a punishment. And Will, I most humbly beg your pardon. I haven't given you the attention that I should have. When we return to Loden Hall it will be to lessons with a proper tutor. For both of you." When she used that tone the boys knew not to argue, but Matt's lower lip stuck out briefly in annoyance. Then Claire asked cheerfully, "Now about that diorama, what exactly did Betcher say about it?" and the conversation moved on to other, less controversial topics.

That afternoon and many afternoons following were even busier than Claire had predicted. Flowers and cards arrived first, even a small bouquet of violets for Claire from "Cousin Walter" that caused her to give a little moue of distaste. She had predicted that the unpleasant man would be a bother and didn't want to welcome him, but Sophie drew the line at that.

"He's family, Claire, and while we may not always like our family, we can't cut 'em. If he comes by, you'll need to be your usual cordial self, no matter how you feel. I won't have any bloodletting in the drawing room. It ain't done."

That comment made Claire laugh and kept her in good humor through the whole afternoon. Walter Thatcher did come, as did several young women with their mothers, and some young men, too, including the handsome Charles Hustisford. He possessed nice manners but had a way of tossing back his head as if to display his perfect profile to maximum advantage that Claire thought might grow annoying over time. Still, it was simply habit and if the affected gesture was his only fault, it could be easily forgiven. He certainly seemed smitten with Cecelia, attentive to her wishes and quick to compliment, all in a perfectly acceptable way. Looking at him, with his good carriage and regal bearing, Claire thought his blonde hair and fair complexion were a wonderful foil to Cecelia's dark beauty.

When she asked Sophie about the Hustisfords, her aunt promptly said, "Old Kent family. Viscount and Lady

Steppington. Been around forever. Don't know of any scandal that's ever touched them. Very high in the instep and proud of their family name. I've heard the fortune ain't what it used to be, but you'd never know it to look at them so that may just be talk. His mother's close to Queen Adelaide, though I can't imagine what they'd have in common. Still, it don't hurt to be on close speaking terms with the queen. They make it a habit to come to town late and for years have announced their arrival with a May ball. Likely you'll get the chance to meet them in a week or two. If their son is dancing attendance on Cecelia, we'll be on their guest list for sure. Their May gathering is always well attended. William and Adelaide came once, and that's rarer than hen's teeth."

All in all, Claire thought, a favorable report. A title but not a grand one since she knew titles continued to make Cecelia uneasy, and if the family fortune wasn't grand, either, it didn't matter as long as there was enough to stay comfortable. Cece had her own money in her own name. In young Hustisford, with his old family name, royal connections, handsome bearing, and respectful manners she might have found her elusive paragon.

April ended in a flurry, entertainments nearly every night and so many invitations they could accept only a small number of all that came their way. The late mornings and afternoons were usually filled with callers and company, and through it all Claire continued to keep her regular schedule. She spent the early mornings with her brothers and would not relinquish that time, no matter how late she had been out the night before.

Symonton, stopping by Millefore Square one late morning, met the three Penwarrens coming back from a walk. The boys were thrilled to see him, and Claire, too, because it reminded her that she intended to ask his advice about arranging a tutor for her brothers. On Symonton's part, he thought Claire looked drawn and had lost a little of the glow he was used to seeing on her face. He sent Will and Matt to pester his groom and went inside with Claire.

"You're looking tired," he said without prologue.

"I had no idea that doing nothing worthwhile could be so fatiguing," Claire admitted with a sigh. "There are constant late nights and a never ending flow of visitors through the afternoon. If I don't get up early, I seldom see the boys and I get nothing done, and living just for pleasure seems too sinful. If it weren't for Cecelia, I'd pack our bags and go home to Loden Valley. I miss our morning walks, Symon."

"As do I," he replied quietly. He met her gaze and held it for a queer little quiet moment that caused her eyes to widen. As a flustered color crept up her cheeks, he broke the silence by asking in an easy tone, "If I read your intentions right, I think you've dropped the order of the paragon onto young Hustisford's shoulders."

Claire had righted herself, the self-conscious, fluttery moment she'd just experienced as a response to the low intensity of Symonton's voice and the flare of some unreadable emotion in his eyes passed so quickly that she almost thought she had imagined it.

"How did you know that? I haven't said a word to anyone but Aunt Sophie. I do like him for Cece. They make such a striking couple."

"Claire, even I would not consider a union with a woman based only on the fact that our coloring contrasted."

"As far as I can tell, Symonton, you wouldn't consider marriage at all."

"I wasn't speaking of marriage," he said dryly, "just a union."

She gave a little gasp mixed with a laugh. "You are very fortunate that I am not easily shocked. Of course, I wouldn't prefer a husband for Cecelia based on the color of his hair. That's not what I meant at all. The young man seems to have all the qualities that would be good for Cece, however, and I admit I do wish she favored him."

"She doesn't then?" Without a by-your-leave Symonton sat down in one of the drawing room chairs, forcing Claire to do the same. He thought it would be only a moment before Sophie found them or the bell rang with a caller, and he was determined to get as much time alone with Claire as he could. He was careful not to come around very often, and when he did, to show as much attention to Cecelia and Sophie as he did to Claire, but despite the few, orchestrated interactions they had, Symonton found it increasingly difficult to think of much else except Claire Penwarren. Found it even more difficult to be in a room with her while able to share only minimal time and superficial conversation. So this rare morning with just the two of them together was a risk, but it was also more precious to him than gold, and he intended to stretch the conversation out for as long as he could.

"I don't know, Symonton. Cece's so quiet. I sometimes get the impression she's uncomfortable with him, but his manners are always impeccable, and she says he's cordial and amusing and never in the least presuming. Perhaps I'm imagining her uneasiness. The only time she's really happy is when your wretched nephew is around." Claire said this with a smile. "I do like Harry, you know. He's genuinely kind and always pleasant and considerate, and so devoted to Cece besides. When she's in the room, he wears an expression somewhere between blinded and dazed."

"But he still won't do for her," the words more of a question than a statement.

"Not a soldier, Symon. I could tolerate a future in the church before the military." She gave him an apologetic smile. "I'm sorry if that makes me seem affected and top heavy. I don't mean it like that. It seemed that Papa was always away on business and while I tried to be everything for Cece, I never felt it was enough. She has always been caught somewhere in between, and I want a happy and stable home life for her. While I don't disagree that Harry has many admirable qualities, I can't wish for Cece to be traipsing behind him around the world or left alone at home to worry about him."

"I see. It is a pity, though, that admirable qualities such as kindness and sincere devotion aren't enough. Will you trade those for stability and security?"

Claire thought she detected criticism and answered tartly, "I don't see why it must be a trade. Cece is so lovely and kind that I have every expectation she can have it all."

"Perhaps she doesn't want it all, Claire."

There was a gentle chiding to his tone that Claire did not miss, but she had already determined that Hustisford, such a pleasant, presentable young man of excellent lineage and — simply as a point of interest, of course, not of *primary* importance in the least — future heir to the Steppington title, was the one to give Cecelia the secure life she deserved. She had no intention of allowing Symonton's disapproval to dim her vision of a bright and happy Cece surrounded by a devoted Charles Hustisford and his admiring parents, Lord and Lady Pennington, so changing the subject and reverting to a bright if somewhat brittle tone she said, "It was serendipitous for you to stop by this morning, Symonton, because I have been meaning to send you a note asking your assistance in finding a tutor suitable for Matt and Will. You know them by now, and you know how different they are, so is it too much to ask to find one man of good education, with a scientific bent and the ability to ride like a Corsair? Perhaps you could help me write the advert." She smiled as she made the suggestion so he would know she was teasing.

"You ask a great deal, Claire."

"I know, but look who it is I ask. I am convinced that if anyone can do *a great deal*, it's you. Next to Aunt Sophie, you should be awarded the prize for knowing the most people at the most levels."

"This is the first I've heard of a prize. I'll need to know what it is before I spend valuable time on the venture."

"The prize is—" Claire hesitated before concluding triumphantly, "—my undying gratitude."

"Not enough, my dear, as ungallant as that may sound, but I might attempt it for a more tangible prize." Claire's brows drew together as she tried to guess his intention, but then she gave up.

"I am too busy for riddles, Symonton, and only spoke figuratively about a prize, but if you insist on one, what must it be?"

The front bell rang at that moment, and he heard Moira open it, then heard the sound of voices. Company at his heels, damn it! Symonton stood to move idly away from Claire and gave her a lazy smile.

"You have visitors and I have an appointment for which I am already late. I'll see if I can uncover an equestrian tutor who also conducts laboratory experiments and we can talk about the prize later." Moira brought a handful of calling cards to Claire, who gave a slight sigh as she stood.

To Moira Claire said, "Please go find Aunt Sophie and tell her we have guests. I'm hardly dressed for entertaining, and she'll have to do duty until I change and find Cecelia."

Distracted from the previous conversation and from Symonton as well, she added, "Thank you, Symonton. I would appreciate it, and here's Aunt Sophie so I must make my escape." She gave him a quick smile and was gone, leaving him to greet Sophie absently and slip out as several people entered the drawing room.

Symonton did not leave unnoticed by those arriving, but because Claire was already gone and only Sophie was in the room, he felt sure there would be no speculative talk at Claire's expense. He had never before spent so much time protecting someone who, when she thought of him at all, thought of him as a cross between fatherly advisor and older brother. He supposed that would have to do for now, but he'd been encouraged by the soft color that crept into her face when they shared that brief, intense, locked look earlier in the morning. He knew that to rush her would have disastrous results, concerned as she was about her sister, her brothers, and her father's arrival from India. Symonton, who had never considered himself an especially patient or tactical man and had never had to be such a man before, discovered a previously unknown core of strategic long-suffering. It was one of several epiphanies he had experienced since devil cat Babu crossed his path so many weeks before.

Claire and Cecelia received the invitation to the Steppingtons' May Ball with mixed feelings. Claire was beside herself with happiness, seeing it as a chance for Charles's parents to see Cecelia at her best. The new gown of Satin Pompadour would be perfect for the occasion, gleaming white embroidered with colorful flowers in jewel tones of blue, green, gold, and purple. Cecelia would look like an Indian princess for sure. Who would not be impressed by her beauty and gracious bearing?

For her part, Cecelia read the invitation with some misgiving. She knew Claire favored young Hustisford and because Cecelia would never willingly have distressed or disappointed her sister, she kept her vague misgivings to herself. While she found Charles perfectly mannered, amusing, and handsome, something—she could not say exactly what— did not ring quite true with him. Cecelia's quiet nature sometimes fooled people into believing she was simple and lacked intelligence, but that was very far from the truth. Like many people of a retiring nature, she was a keen observer of her environment and had developed a perceptive sense of intuition that was seldom wrong. It accounted for her ability to say exactly the right thing at exactly the right time to placate or distract, a talent her family recognized and appreciated. She was not completely comfortable with Charles Hustisford, but she tried to blame the discomfort on her heart's desire to be with only one person and her complete lack of interest in anyone whose name was not Harry Macapee. For Claire's sake Cecelia would endure the suffocating social schedule of London in May, but she would have been much happier back at Loden Hall, Harry sitting on the stool in front of her with a skein of wool wrapped around his hands, watching her with unabashed pleasure and neither of them saying a word. That was a heaven Claire simply did not understand.

"Oh, Cece, my dear!" exclaimed Claire, seeing her sister dressed for the May ball. "How beautiful you look! How absolutely dead-on beautiful!" The embroidered flowers of Cecelia's dress seemed to have a glow all their own, the silk threads picking up the soft shine of candlelight. Everything about Cece seemed to glow, black hair, creamy brown skin, wide, dark eyes, cheeks and teeth and lips all smooth and flawless, nothing pastel or pale about her.

The evening started out wonderfully. Claire was happy to hear from Harry Macapee that Lady Pasturson had finally arrived in town, although she had chosen to spend that particular evening with her daughter and son-in-law. Because Charles Hustisford had been dancing noticeable attendance on Cecelia from their arrival—to Harry's poorly hidden dismay—Claire found herself in sympathetic charity with the young man. He was such a pleasant, handsome young man, so obviously (and understandably) smitten with Cece and looking as woebegone as a lost puppy every time any other man led her to the dance floor. It wasn't Harry's fault that he would have a military future; second sons often had to accept choices that might not be their first inclination. Claire watched Harry dancing with Cecelia without a quiver of misgiving because after a brief introduction to Charles's parents at the beginning of the evening, she had watched Viscount and Lady Steppington pause on the room's perimeter more than once as the night progressed to observe their son with Cecelia. They must surely see and approve the stunning couple Charles and Cecelia made. All in all, Claire was satisfied with the evening's progression.

Symonton, also present, casually made his way to Claire's side as she stood behind her aunt's chair watching the activity with a happy look on her face that gave his heart a peculiarly painful ache. He wished she would look at him with that same gratifyingly joyful look, but he stoically accepted that he had nothing to do with the obvious and palpable delight that glowed from her eyes.

He arrived to stand before Sophie and Claire simultaneously with Walter Thatcher, who remarked off-handedly, "Oh, it's you Symonton. Beg your pardon. I'm here to take my cousin off for the next dance."

Symonton, after giving Thatcher a wordless look that went from crown to toe, said with detached disdain, "Really? I think you must be confused, which I understand can be a natural effect of having one's waist too tightly constricted."

Claire gave a sudden and stifled cough, put a delicate handkerchief to her lips and begged pardon vaguely, but her eyes twinkled at Symonton.

"I'm afraid Symonton is right, Sir Walter, at least about the confusion, since I am not allowed to discuss the effects of waist restriction with the same abandon.as his lordship. It would not be quite proper, I fear. The dance just ended was supposed to be ours, and I can only thank you for allowing me to join my aunt on the sidelines to enjoy a brief respite." Claire looked at her dance card and said, "This one, in fact, belongs to Symonton." She stepped forward and put her hand on Symonton's arm.

"I don't think—" blustered Thatcher, but Claire and Symonton had already disappeared into the crowd on the dance floor.

"You can be astonishingly reprehensible sometimes, Symonton," Claire murmured from Symonton's side.

"You didn't seem especially squeamish about the truth," he retorted, both of them conversing at the same time they smiled at the friends and acquaintances they passed. "Tell me that you didn't appreciate me rescuing you from your pompous cousin and I'll take you back to him immediately and admit my error."

"Don't you dare. Only to you can I admit that I find it increasingly difficult to tolerate the man's company. He uses our distant family connection to lecture me about my unfortunate managing ways and to make patronizing comments about Cecelia. It's all I can do to keep from slamming the door in his face whenever I hear his voice begging entrance with that tone of loathsome condescension, as if he deserves welcome just because our grandmothers were sisters." They came to a stop and took their positions for the next set.

"Speaking of sisters, Cecelia looks especially stunning tonight, Claire."

"She does, doesn't she? I've noticed Charles's parents dwelling on her more than once this evening." Claire looked directly at Symonton as she spoke, her delight so tangible that he felt it like the warmth of a flame on his skin. Claire happy was the most glorious thing Symonton had ever seen. "I'm sure they must be feeling extraordinarily fortunate that their son has developed a tendre for a girl as lovely and kind and well-bred as Cece."

Claire was soon to discover that the Steppingtons felt nothing of the sort. She and Cecelia came out of one of the rooms used by the ladies to refresh their toilettes, the entrance discreetly covered with a screen of potted palms, and Claire had pulled her sister to the side momentarily to rearrange Cecelia's shawl across her shoulders.

"Perfect," Claire whispered with a smile, and then the two young women stopped still as statues. On the other side of the palms two people were having a subdued but forceful discussion that, because of some acoustic peculiarity of the corner in which they stood, Claire could hear as clearly as if the participants were speaking from a podium directly in front of her.

"You have been telling Charles to find an heiress since he was in drawstrings," the man hissed, "and now that he has, you're kicking up at his choice." Claire recognized Lord Steppington's distinctive lisp and knew that the heiress to which he referred must be Cecelia. She felt suddenly chilled and looked about for a way to pull Cecelia away without anyone noticing. There was no escape, however. The small crowd of chatting women behind them would not let them retreat and they must either walk out past the couple or wait behind the tall palms until the speakers departed. At Lady Steppington's response, walking out past her and her husband ceased to be an option.

The woman's voice was ice cold. "I will sell my jewels before I see my son walk down the aisle with some dark heathen woman that has the shameless nerve to ingratiate herself into our family. Imagine a picture of her hanging on the wall next to mine. Wouldn't that give future generations cause for gossip and laughter? I would be appalled to introduce her to the queen as my daughter-in-law and only think what Charles's children would look like! Don't bother telling me she comes from the Penwarrens. There is no blood line strong enough to dilute that dark stain."

At those cutting, malicious, disdainful words, Claire knew a fury so strong she thought the top of her head must blow off. She looked quickly at Cecelia, saw that all the color had drained from her sister's face, and put a hand quickly on her arm.

The man spoke wearily. "Pity it's not the older sister. Their money may come from trade and tea, but the creditors wouldn't complain. I'll call Charles off tomorrow."

"You will call him off tonight," the woman snapped back. "It's disgraceful to see them together any longer than necessary. I will not have that woman in my family." Claire heard a rustle of cloth and then nothing. The two must have departed in search of their son.

She found her hands were shaking badly and it was Cecelia who took them into hers.

"It's all right, Claire. Don't look like that. I knew something was not quite right about Charles, that there was something false just below the surface, but I couldn't say what. He was always so perfect in his attentions but there was never any substance to him. I don't care a whit about him or his parents, and I don't care about what they said."

But Claire was finding it difficult to listen. How dare they demean Cecelia, speak of her in that disparaging way, as if she weren't the daughter of a princess and an earl, as if Cecelia couldn't trace her mother's lineage back long before there was ever a London or a Steppington or a Hustisford! She would tell her hostess just that; tell her how very ill bred and common it was to speak of someone using the tone and terms she had used, and an invited guest in their home at that; tell her how pathetic her intellect and education must be; tell her Charles would have been the privileged one and his family fortunate to include Cecelia; tell her Cecelia would have been doing them the favor and the Penwarrens were the ones who would not allow their blood lines to be contaminated with the likes of the Steppingtons! Claire would say all that in a way that would not be misunderstood or soon forgotten.

Cecelia, seeing the glaze of fury and distress in her sister's eyes, was genuinely concerned. It wasn't the first time she had overheard such comments about herself, and she had ceased to be bothered by prejudice and bad manners a long time ago. Despite her quiet nature, Cecelia was as strong minded as her sister, proud and knowledgeable of her heritage and certain of her place in the world. She usually hid such comments from Claire or made a laughing, dismissive remark about people's ignorance, knowing that to do otherwise would distress her sister. She would always picture Claire boldly moving from corner to corner with a stool raised over her head, willing to risk her own life to protect her sister. Claire's love ran deep and true, and to keep most of the hurtful comments from Claire was only to protect her. The look on Claire's face and the deep anger in her eyes were painful for Cecelia to see.

"But I care," responded Claire tersely. She put a quick palm against her sister's cheek, "and I won't hear you so abused. Go back directly to Aunt Sophie and gather our wraps. I will express my displeasure to Lady Steppington and then we will leave immediately. Do you think I am afraid of them?"

"I don't think that would be a wise course," Cecelia began, but Claire had already stepped away and was looking around the large, crowded room for her host and hostess. Cecelia felt helpless to know what to do. Instinctively she realized that Claire's intentions would make matters worse not better, but she had never seen Claire like this, shaking with fury, intractable, and merciless. Cecelia started to walk briskly toward the opposite side where Sophie sat and looked up as someone took her arm. It was Symonton, and she felt a great wave of relief. Of course. Symonton. He would know exactly what to do. Claire was oblivious to his feelings, but Cecelia, in her quiet and observant way, had watched him watch Claire for many weeks now and knew he would do anything for her sister.

"What is it?" he asked, not bothering with preliminaries. Cecelia's usual warm complexion was ashen, and he had seen Claire go in the opposite direction of her sister, her posture unnaturally tense and her expression rigid. Something was surely amiss.

Cecelia told him the story quickly and without embellishment. "I've never seen her like this and she wouldn't listen to a word I said. She seemed—oh, I don't know how to explain—she seemed incapable of hearing me at all. Can you stop her, my lord? I don't care about me. I could live happily at Loden Hall all my life, but it will hurt Claire's prospects and our father's reputation if she follows through with her intention."

Symonton knew Cecelia was right in her assessment of the situation. He turned away from her, saw Claire's bright head across the room, slipped outside through the nearest open door, and hurried along the covered verandah that traversed two sides of the large house, reentering through another door that put him right on Claire's heels. Stretching out a hand he managed to grasp her upper arm firmly from behind, bringing her to an abrupt stop. She tried to shake loose with an impatient jerk, and when she could not free herself looked back with an expression of ferocious irritation on her face until she recognized Symonton.

Claire said his name but curtly and without her usual welcoming warmth. "I can't talk now. Please let me go."

Even he, experienced in all matters female, had been taken aback by the look on Claire's face, everything soft and bright he'd come to expect replaced by a fury that tightened her mouth and reduced the warmth of her eyes to black ice. So might a lioness look on the prowl for supper for its young, he thought, and tightened his grip on Claire's arm.

"I think not. Step outside with me." He knew that taking her—compelling her, to be more accurate—outside with him was a risk. People would notice and perhaps comment, but compared to the alternative it was a risk he was willing to take.

"Now is not the time, Symonton."

"Now is exactly the time," he retorted in a low, firm voice. "You are being tiresome, my girl, and people are beginning to look at us. Step outside with me. Now." He could tell that she was annoyed with this interruption to her plans—she was a woman whose life was made up of plans and good intentions, after all—but she allowed herself to be pulled outside. The night was unusually warm for early May, with a cloudy sky and hazy moon that portended rain. Fortunately, the music had just started up for a popular dance and their particular section of the verandah was empty except for the two of them.

"What do you want?" she asked crossly when he finally released her arm.

Symonton stood facing her from a little distance, keeping his back to the open door, shielding her from the view of anyone who might walk by and glance out.

"Cecelia told me what happened. She asked me to keep you from making an idiot of yourself."

"You didn't hear them, Symon!" The anger and pain in Claire's voice struck him with the force of a physical blow. He could see that her hands, clenching a bright paisley shawl tightly about her shoulders, were shaking. Her voice shook, too. "You didn't hear them, Symon," she repeated, "the horrid, horrid things they said about Cecelia. How dare they!"

Like Cecelia, Symonton had not imagined that Claire had such a deep core of passion in her. He was used to seeing her calm and levelheaded, interspersed with the occasional pique, perhaps, but always sensible enough to laugh at her own small tempers. How could he have imagined this Claire, this woman blazing with outraged purpose? After thought, however, he supposed he shouldn't be surprised. She was so protective of her family that any threat or insult to them must certainly produce just such a fierce reaction.

"My dear," he said gently, "people say horrid things about other people more often than not, and especially the people in the room beyond us."

"To judge Cece without knowing her, to judge her based only on her appearance and to do it in such a terrible, spiteful way is wicked!"

Another place or time, Symonton would have folded Claire into his arms for comfort, raised her shaking hands to his mouth and kissed each finger until she calmed. He knew he could not do that here and now, but the urge was powerful enough that he retreated a step in self-control.

"Certainly it's wicked, but people do wicked things all the time, Claire. *You* would be doing something just as wrong, if not exactly wicked, to create a scene in the middle of this famous occasion. At this moment the room holds the most important people in London."

"I don't care about that. I want, I need, to tell Lady Steppington how despicable I find her behavior."

"You think you don't care because your temper is raw and your emotions high, but if you have ever trusted me, Claire, trust me now and believe me. If you make any kind of hysterical scene this evening, if you act in any way that is other than pleasant and courteous, you will do lasting damage to your sister, your brothers, and your father's ascension to the title. People have long memories and enjoy scandal. By the time the story passes through town, you won't recognize it. It will be much, much worse than the true occurrence, and it won't be your hostess who is faulted. She will become the victim and you will be virago and villain."

Claire stared at Symonton enrapt and listening intently now to every word. He watched the fierce emotion on her face slowly fade, saw it slip behind her eyes to be purposefully replaced by a calculated look of weary amusement she had dredged up from some deep inner resource of strength and character.

"Surely not both virago *and* villain, Symonton," she said finally, lightly, almost in the voice he was accustomed to hearing. "Even I could not sustain both of those roles with equal vigor."

At that moment the Marquis of Symonton, a man that had managed to elude the peculiarly glorious pain of true love for a full six and thirty years, realized how deeply and completely he loved this woman, this Claire Penwarren, this magnificent creature standing before him. Gone were his musings that he was a medical abnormality unable to feel meaningful emotion or deep attachment. He loved everything about her, that dear face and rather unassuming figure, her humor and her passion and the loyalty and love that were as natural a part of her as hazel eyes and auburn hair. He was a man in love for the first time in his life. For the last time, too. In his own way Symonton was as surprised as any acquaintance would have been to know that his affections had finally settled on a spinster a decade out of the schoolroom who had been raised in the wilds of India, but there it was. For reasons he was not yet ready or able to articulate, no woman would ever suit him except Claire Penwarren. In his mind, she already belonged to him in heart and spirit, and someday, God willing—so strong was his rush of awareness that even in the middle of this drama the imagining had the power to arouse him—his in body, as well. That passion flashing from her eyes should not be wasted on spinsterhood.

When Claire went to move past him to rejoin the crowd inside, Symonton shook his head.

"No. You stay here and let me go in first. I'll say you have a headache and send Sophie to you. She should lead you back into the room."

"Why ever for?" Her tone was one of utter bafflement.

"Why do you think?"

Claire pondered a moment before her eyes lit up in understanding. "How very silly, Symonton!"

She had the unconscious ability to humble him at the most unexpected moments, he thought ruefully as she continued, "I suppose it's because we are out here alone together and someone might think that you and I—"

He waited for her to finish the thought, but when it became apparent she had no intention of putting the ridiculous notion into words, he said, "Yes. One can't be too careful, Claire, not with this crowd, and I do have something of a reputation. Once begun, rumors take on a life of their own and the more salacious, the faster they fly." She put a hand up to rub her temple in an unconscious gesture.

"What foolishness it all is but, of course, you're right as usual. I wasn't thinking." She realized what she said and added without diffidence, "I haven't been thinking for a while now, Symonton, so thank you for intervening. My actions would have been the height of foolishness and impropriety and you're right that they would only have hurt Cece more. I already have too much to beg her pardon for."

"Why should you need to ask your sister's pardon for anything?" His question held a peremptory challenge but he did not like seeing her meek, too out of character for the Claire Penwarren he knew. And loved.

"Because it was my ambition and insensitivity that brought her to this, and I am deeply ashamed of myself. I'll tell her so as soon as we're alone."

"My dear, you have never done one thing that hasn't had the best and most generous of intentions."

Her lips tightened with unmistakable disdain before she replied, "I believe the words *she meant well* are some of the most pathetic in the English language. Never mind me, Symon. It sometimes takes me a while to learn a lesson, but once I learn it I never forget it. Please go away and get Aunt Sophie so I can complete the charade. I will reenter with a hand to my brow and I will rest long enough for my throbbing head to recover its equilibrium. Actually, that's not so far from the truth right now. My head is starting to throb."

Symonton carefully watched Claire from a distance for the rest of the evening. If he had not seen her shaking with rage and hurt, had not heard the pain in her voice or seen those laughing eyes blinded by guilt and unshed tears, he would not have believed the incident ever happened. The Penwarrens stayed another hour at least, laughing and dancing until Claire finally pleaded a return of her headache. She made it a point to seek out her hostess for a pretty farewell before they departed, her smile seeming as genuine as her appreciation of the evening's activities. If Claire's palm itched to smack that superior look from Lady Steppington's long-jawed face, no one would ever have guessed so from her calm expression and complimentary words.

Cecelia stopped by Symonton's side on her way out. "Thank you, my lord. I don't know what you said or how you did it, but thank you."

Symonton had the bewildering sense that he'd just experienced a reversal of sorts: a mature Cecelia expressing her concern for her sister and her appreciation for Claire's rescue. Perhaps there was more to this younger sister than he had thought.

"She just loves so very deeply," Cecelia said, adding softly as she turned away from him, "It is both her greatest strength and what makes her most vulnerable."

Robert Septimus Louis Carlisle, Marquis of Symonton, Baron of several lesser regions, and man in love understood with exquisite clarity exactly what Cecelia meant.

Chapter 7

*B*y the time the Penwarren women finally left the Steppingtons' grand but apparently under-funded London home, Claire truly did have a headache. *A fitting penance,* she thought as the coach rattled across the rough streets, *for my rash temper and the poor example I set for my sister. If anything, I need to learn from Cecelia,* who seemed completely untouched by the rude comments they had overheard and whose only concern was for Claire's well-being.

Sophie, Cecelia, and Claire spoke little on the way home. Sophie knew something untoward had occurred as soon as Symonton had appeared in front of her, looking like the epithet sometimes used to describe him—the consummate Ice Man— cool blue eyes, chilly demeanor, the flat planes of his lean face frozen into an expression of supreme sangfroid. Even Sophie found the man somewhat frightening when he wore that look. His message sent her immediately in search of Claire, surprised to hear that her elder niece was feeling indisposed. When she found her, Claire was staring out at the dark gardens, her arms wrapped around herself as if warding off a chill. To Sophie the girl seemed more distressed or troubled than ill, and for a moment Sophie wondered if someone had taken improper liberties with her niece, done something to frighten or agitate her. Watching her through the remainder of the evening, however, she decided that was not the case.

To one who hadn't lived with Claire closely for the past several weeks, it might have appeared that she truly suffered from a headache miraculously cured by a glass of tepid punch, but Sophie knew that whatever had occurred to upset Claire, a headache had no part in it. The girl had the constitution of a horse and more energy than was fashionable for young women to possess. Something else had happened. She couldn't guess what but despite their short acquaintance, Sophie felt a strong affection and concern for Claire. If the girl chose to share what had driven the color from her cheeks and put that unnatural glaze in her eyes, Sophie would try to put it right. If not, well, they would continue exactly as before, admitting to nothing. Goodness knew she'd had years of experience covering over catastrophes and scandals when Thomas was alive. She would wait and watch and take her lead from Claire.

Once home, Cecelia went off to bed after giving Claire a wordless soft kiss on the cheek. Claire tried to follow her sister's example, but once in bed she lay staring into the darkness, reliving in her mind's eyes the events of the evening until she decided that if she ever wanted to fall sleep again she must say what she needed to say to Cecelia regardless of the hour.

She pushed open her sister's door and said, "Cece?" into the black room. Hearing a murmur that she chose to interpret as invitation, Claire entered, stubbed her toe against the foot of a small table, stifled a word she would have said only because she was tired and annoyed with herself, and limped her way closer to the bed. "Cece, are you awake?"

Cecelia sat up, too groggy and too kind to respond that if she hadn't been awake before she certainly was *now*, for heaven's sake, and managed to ask, "What is it, Claire?" with credible interest.

Looking like a pale ghost in the flickering shadows of her candle, Claire came to sit at the edge of the bed, set the candle down on the bedside table with deliberate care, and folded both hands in her lap.

Babu padded quietly behind Claire into the room and leapt lightly onto the extra pillow next to Cecelia, kneading his paws as if he were making bread and purring loudly. How accommodating that his two favorite humans should decide to have a talk in the middle of the night, his very favorite time for activity! Perhaps they were trainable after all.

Claire took a breath and spoke in one long and uninterrupted sentence. "Cece, I can't sleep until I beg your pardon for being a fool and a terrible sister I should have paid more attention to your opinions and listened more carefully to you instead I treated you like you were still a little girl how arrogant that I should think I know what's best for everyone I was wrong to try to make you want what I wanted for you can you ever forgive me?" Only when she reached the end of the speech did her voice crack.

Cece's response was immediate and sincere. "Claire, you are not a fool or a terrible sister or arrogant—well, sometimes you might be perceived as arrogant but only in the most loving way—and while I don't believe there is anything to forgive, if you can't sleep without my forgiveness, please be assured that you have it. Now go to bed. I really can't stay awake any longer."

Claire felt a wave of relief, the words all said and Cecelia not angry—but, of course, when had *that* ever happened?—or apparently affected at all by the vile things they had overheard earlier. She stood, suddenly feeling as tired as Cecelia sounded. When she reached the connecting door to her own room, she heard Cece say her name and turned back with concern. Second thoughts? Wounded, after all? But it was nothing of the sort.

"Only the words of the people I love are important, Claire. Those are the only words with the power to hurt me. Don't let what happened tonight keep you awake any longer."

Claire, mollified and blinking back sudden and inexplicable tears, climbed into her bed and slept well into the morning, dreamily ignoring the rain that pattered against the windows. She lay there in a semi-state of pleasant slumber until Moira knocked hesitantly on her door.

There had been considerable discussion in the kitchen before it came to that.

"She's always up by now," Moira said to Feastwell, chewing on her lower lip with worry. "She seemed all right when I helped her undress last night, though a little more quiet than usual. You don't think she's ill, do you?"

Mrs. Feastwell, used to setting out early coffee for Claire, had turned to Crayton

"She wouldn't take her usual walk this morning, what with the rain, so she may just have decided to sleep later, but I don't suppose it would hurt to check on her and be sure she wasn't taken ill in the night. What do you think, Crayton?"

The housekeeper gave final approval and so Moira disappeared to knock timidly on Claire's bedchamber door, then turn the knob and peer inside.

"Are you all right, Miss? It's well past your usual breakfast time."

Moira was surprised to see Claire up and dressed but sitting motionless on the edge of the bed. When she looked over at Moira, the girl thought Claire really was ill, her face drawn and sad and smudged shadows under her eyes.

Then Claire stood, stretched, and declared cheerfully, "I'm fine, just a slugabed this morning, Moira. Too many late nights, I expect. I'll come down with you now. Coffee sounds exactly what I need. Are the boys up?"

Claire seemed herself again, a little pale perhaps but pleasantly in charge as usual, and Moira thought she had been mistaken about her mistress looking sad. It must have been the dreary reflection of a rainy morning she had seen on Claire's face.

In a way Moira truly was mistaken, for Claire was not a woman given to moods or melancholy and it would not have been accurate to say she was sad. She had awakened that morning, grateful beyond words that Symonton had interrupted her furious plans. She knew that if he had not done so, she would have awakened full of regret instead, having done damage to her own and her family's reputation, wishing she could turn back the clock. Thanks to her friend, no such damage had been done. She needed to express her gratitude properly and thought she would write him a note that morning to tell him so.

Beyond the gratitude, however, was a deep sense of humility. She had been wrong about Charles Hustisford and his parents, and with the fair-mindedness that was so much a part of her nature, Claire realized she might be equally as wrong about Harry Macapee. All she had planned and dreamed of for Cecelia, everything about which she had once been so certain, was turned upside down. She had been wrong on several levels, but with typical firmness of purpose Claire promised herself that if Harry genuinely loved Cecelia and her sister returned the affection, she would do nothing to stand in the way of the connection. Papa would arrive within the next few weeks, and he would meet Harry and make the final decision. Whatever happened, Cecelia had grown into a self-possessed and perceptive woman, had, in fact, conducted herself with greater maturity than Claire the previous evening regardless of their ages, and it was ludicrous for Claire to continue to act as if her increased years made her so wise that she could look into the future and determine what was best for her sister's happiness. She must cease picturing Cece as a little girl that needed to be protected and learn to respect her as an adult woman, one able to know her own heart and follow her own course.

Claire told all this to Cecelia later with Aunt Sophie also at the table. "I've only ever wanted what's best for you," Claire concluded, "but I realize you are a grown woman capable of managing your own life. I will always be here for you, and I can't help it if I volunteer my opinion once in a while—I can't reform *that* much—but my chief duty and obligation now is to love you, just love you, my dear, which I hope you know I will always do."

At Claire's final words Cecelia, wearing a rare wide smile, stood up quickly to come around the table and give her sister a hug.

The Honourable Charles Hustisford never returned to Millefore Square and no one missed him. Claire only wished she could rid herself of her cousin Walter as thoroughly, but his skull seemed to be as thick as a brick and she could not detect any perceptive ability in him whatsoever. She was confident that if she painted *WALTER, GO AWAY AND STAY AWAY* on the front door in bold capital letters, he would look at it with his usual dense smugness, wonder dimly, "What's that all about, then?" and pick up the knocker.

Except for her distant relative's too frequent presence, Claire was able to relax and lick her wounds. She let Aunt Sophie and Cecelia deal with callers and spent more time with her brothers. For a few days following her outburst at the May Ball, she felt curiously lethargic and quiet, but the mood didn't last and slowly everyone in the house began to breathe and act normally again. Everyone, even Babu although he'd never admit it, had felt uncertain and vaguely unhappy while Claire was not herself, and it wasn't until she was heard humming in the hallway or seen picking up her skirts to chase Matthew down the steps that people gave a collective exhale of relief. Their world had righted.

Symonton stayed away for a week trying to right his world, as well. He had his own emotions to deal with, and he wanted to give Claire time to recover, besides. He thought she had been as surprised and shaken by the depth of her anger and the ferociousness of her feelings as anyone. She had written him a pretty thank you on crisp engraved paper and sprayed it lightly with rosewater. Symonton couldn't bring himself to part with the missive once he read it. His valet, who with the finely tuned talent for quiet observation that men of his profession were noted for, saw the delicate card and envelope slipped into a pocket one day or tucked into a boot the next, but he was wise enough to say nothing. Geoffrey had been with Symonton for over a decade and at first supposed the blush-colored note was from a new paramour of his lordship's but on second thought couldn't figure out how and when that alliance would have been established. Since their arrival in town, Symonton had frequented none of the places where one met that particular type of female companion. In fact, there hadn't been a woman in his master's life for months, unless he counted that pleasant Miss Penwarren from Loden Hall whom he'd met this spring during their stay in the country. A very nice young lady, of course, but too fresh-faced, green, and sassy, begging her pardon, for his lordship, who preferred companions of more opulent beauty, specific experience, and practiced skills. Geoffrey found the present goings on mysterious but was too much the consummate valet to say anything. It would all work itself out, even if he had never seen this particular mood in his lordship before. Perhaps there were money problems. Geoffrey hoped not. He valued his position and actually liked his lordship. It would be hard to find another place that suited him so well.

Symonton finally decided the time was right to drop by the Penwarrens one morning only to find he had been preceded by his sister and his nephew.

"Symonton!" cried Margaret happily, rising as if it were her own parlor and going to kiss him lightly on the cheek. "I haven't seen you in such a while. I feel overlooked and ignored. When did you plan to come and visit Alice? She asks about you every day."

Symonton wished his niece were more like her mother, not the stammering, whey-faced young woman that she was, and he did not desire or intend to spend any time with her at all. Yet when he opened his mouth to tell Margaret precisely that, he saw Claire smiling at him, her glance sending the clear message that she had overheard Margaret's question, read his mind, heard his thoughts about his niece, and anticipated an unacceptable response. At least, that's what her look seemed to say to him, both her brows raised in a question and her head tilted ever so slightly to the side in the exact same manner he had seen her use on her brothers when they needed a gentle chastisement. It hardly seemed fair when he had only *thought* the words, but there was no more use his grumbling about the situation than the twins protesting it. Neither would have had any effect on Claire's mute correction and Symonton found himself saying to his sister, "Would tomorrow do? I didn't know if she was up to company." He gave Claire a slight, irascible glare but she, refusing to be cowed, smiled back her approval.

Their wordless exchange had taken only seconds, but Margaret had caught it all and was so amazed to have missed what was blossoming right under her nose that she had to sit down rather abruptly to steady herself. Her brother, very dear to her but with a deserved reputation for being both spoiled and indolent, and Claire Penwarren with her brisk good nature and unspoiled smile? Who could have imagined an attraction between them? The idea delighted Margaret beyond words. Robert should have set up his nursery years ago and despite his sometimes chilly reception to her affection, she often thought he was the loneliest person she knew. It would be interesting to watch how the matter progressed, interesting and no doubt entertaining, as well.

Symonton wandered over by Claire to murmur, "I believe I've found just the instructor for the boys" and when her face lit with pleasure instantly regretted that he hadn't uncovered a dozen instructors if such a delightful response was the reward for locating only one.

"Have you? *You* are the paragon, Symonton. I know you wouldn't have said anything if you didn't think it was a good match."

"Come out riding with me in the morning," he invited. "I have a new pair that I want to try out, and it will be perfectly unremarkable for you to join me for a turn around the park. I'll tell you about him then."

For reasons she did not try to identify, Claire looked forward to the morning ride with more pleasure than she had to any of the entertainments of the past month. Symonton had taken on the status of a family friend from their March morning walks back in Sussex, and what had occurred at the May Ball only strengthened her regard for him. No Ice Man to her but a kind friend who offered welcome advice and real assistance without patronizing her or expecting something in return. She never felt constrained in his company or felt she must somehow charm or manipulate him out of a bad mood or into a good one, even if that were possible. He was simply and unapologetically who he was, and she felt nothing but relief and comfort in his company. Sometimes she thought that the only time she truly relaxed was when she was at his side. How and when their relationship had grown into such a friendship she couldn't have said, but she wouldn't have traded or changed it for the world.

Society's ambivalent view of the man, simultaneously admiring and uneasy, was of no importance to Claire. She knew Symonton for his good sense and objective viewpoint and had come to realize that when he strayed too close to unbecoming traits, it was usually for his own defense. No one other than his sister would have given credit to Claire's conclusion, but she knew it to be true and knowing it, sometimes found herself—as ridiculous as it seemed—as protective over Symonton as she was over her siblings.

It was just one further mental step, then, to tell herself that sisterly was exactly how she felt about him. With that deduction Claire chose to ignore with blithe determination the emotion she sometimes felt at odd moments in the man's presence, something that churned low in her stomach and possessed the ability to cause a brief breathlessness on her part. The particular emotion was new to her and she was intelligent enough to recognize it was not in the least sisterly, but that was as far as she was willing to explore.

When Symonton came for her the next morning, she stopped at the horses long enough to ask, "Has Matt seen these black beauties yet?" and at his answer added, "I thought not because I'm sure we would have heard about it morning to night if he had. They're beautiful beasts, Symon. I don't pretend to have an eye for horse flesh like yours, but even I can tell they're top of the trees."

Claire wore a dress the color of strawberries with a little flounced cape over her shoulders and a broad brimmed straw hat with a white feather that curved down to caress her cheek. When she looked at him like that, her eyes so friendly and that warm smile directed straight at him, his chest felt constricted and for a moment he couldn't have said a coherent word if his life depended on it. He'd always thought every poetic description of love to be complete nonsense, but God help him, here he was as love struck as a schoolboy. None of his acquaintances would have believed it; he could hardly credit it himself.

They had no sooner started off when Claire demanded, "Don't tease, Symonton, it's unkind. Tell me this instant about the teacher you've found."

"His name is Mr. Adam Freeman. He's been with Lord Stanhope for several years, but he's not an old man by any stretch. There are four Stanhope sons so there was plenty to keep Freeman busy and as far as I can tell all the Stanhope sons emerged with solid educations and good manners. The youngest boy is off to university now, though, and Stanhope, who has the highest regard for Freeman, offered him a stipend and a permanent home with them. To Freeman's credit, he refused, said he enjoyed teaching and wanted to continue and asked Stanhope's assistance in finding another position."

"Will he do for both Will and Matt, do you think? He sounds older than I would have wished."

"I think if he can handle four Stanhope sons all a year apart, he can handle your two brothers. I took some time to meet him and found him to be of impressive intellect without being stuffy. He's forty years old and an excellent pugilist. I've seen him at practice. " Claire gave her little crow of laughter.

"You are amazing, Symonton! If I didn't believe that you knew how important this was to me, I'd be tempted to think you were making all that up to tease. Mr. Freeman sounds too, too perfect." The glow of pleasure he felt at her happiness did not show anywhere on his face.

Instead, without looking at her, he responded, "You must meet him yourself, of course, but I don't think you'll be disappointed. Shall I ask him to visit Millefore Square?"

"Yes, please, and if he suits, I will have accomplished at least one objective and we can at last go home."

"Much of the season remains, Claire."

"Cecelia is tired of it and, truthfully, so am I. You know better than anyone that I have not been at my best lately, and I'm usually the most even-tempered of women. I must be more of a blue-stocking than I thought because lately I've longed for no more exciting an evening than to curl up on the settee with the latest novel. I've neglected the boys, too; so much so that I'm alarmed at their conduct. They're like a garden that must be tended and tilled regularly or it reverts to its wild state. Papa should be here next month, and I haven't finished the bedchambers at Loden Hall. He'd be unhappy and disappointed if he saw them in their present condition of threadbare carpets and dusty bed coverings, everything done in drab brown and greens. I know my papa and he has a sophisticated eye for color and fabric. What's there now would give him nightmares. I have plenty to do, Symon, and I find six weeks of fripperies and self-indulgence to be all I can tolerate."

"Ever the family conscience." She laughed at the description.

"I didn't mean to make myself sound like that, especially sitting beside you. You know very well how unsuited I am for that role, but I want the hall to look nice for Papa. He has so many affectionate memories of his home, and it would be a shock if he saw the place as it is now. Don't you feel that way about Symonton?"

"Affectionate memories, you mean? No, I can't say that I do. My mother died before I was in pants and my father was not a man of much cheer or good humor. Symonton suited his bleak temperament so he kept it dark and plain."

"But surely you could change that now if you chose."

"I think the place as it is continues to suit my bleak temperament."

She would not be drawn into such a self-serving discussion but said with matter-of-fact advice, "Then you need a wife who will renovate the place in spite of your perceived bleak and wanting temperament. I find it curious that you don't have a wife, Symonton." The rather improper comment slipped out before she realized what exactly she'd said, and she took a quick side glimpse to see if his mouth had tightened in the understated but very effective way he had of expressing his disapproval. She was relieved that his lips — he had a very fine mouth, she thought suddenly and rather disjointedly, full-lipped and more expressive than one expected to find in a man — tilted upward slightly. His version of a smile.

"Because of my social standing you mean?" he asked dryly.

"Because of your advanced years," she retorted, "or is it only females who must give a defensive explanation of their unmarried status? Despite my intentions to the contrary, I sometimes feel an obligation to detail the reasons for my spinsterhood."

"I don't need to articulate an explanation. I told you recently that society has a long memory so anyone who was here twelve years ago understands my bachelor status." Claire turned to look at his profile.

"I was sixteen, on the other side of the world, and preoccupied with a widowed father and an eight-year-old sister then, Symonton, so I have no idea what you're talking about."

"When I was twenty-four I met the woman of my dreams," his lordship explained thoughtfully, keeping his eyes on the path before them, "or so I thought. She was two years older than I, petite and black haired, and she told me she was a widow."

"Ah." Claire spoke the one syllable and waited, the sway of the carriage offering the same rhythm as a cradle.

"The banns were published and the announcement sent to the paper," Symonton continued. "Neither my father nor my sister was pleased, but I would not hear one word against Ophelia."

"Oh, Symonton, not *Ophelia,* not really."

He turned to glare at her. "It was not a stage comedy, Claire."

"Of course, not. Not if her name was Ophelia," responded Claire reasonably and was rewarded with another quick look and a further upward tilt to his mouth. She hadn't liked the self-deprecating, bitter tone that had crept into his voice. "Since you remain unattached with admirable determination, I gather the story did not end well."

"She neglected to mention the one small detail that her husband was still alive. Her plan was to come into my inheritance and maintain relationships with both her husbands, one who had a fortune and the other who had her heart. I was the one with the fortune. My father, who hired the investigative work, delighted in telling me the whole sordid story. Its effect on me didn't matter to him. He had retired to Cornwall and was only concerned about the family name, not my particular circumstance."

Claire's heart gave a little turn as Symonton spoke. She had thought early on that he hadn't always been the Ice Man and sometimes wondered if there was a deeper reason for cultivating so frosty an image other than predatory society mothers. Now she understood.

"How trying for you, Symonton! Is that what turned your hair prematurely white?" He sent her another stern look, caught her sympathetic and solicitous eye, and laughed out loud.

"You are incorrigible. Don't you care at all about my broken heart?"

She patted his arm with a quick, affectionate, involuntary gesture of sympathy before she said, "Of course, I do. You've been a wonderful friend to me, and I'd like to put your Ophelia and my cousin Walter in a large barrel and roll them both downhill, but you can't wish not to have discovered her duplicity. Think how much worse it would have been had you actually wed. The idea makes even me shudder and I am quite stout-hearted. I'm selfish besides. If you and Ophelia were married, you would have a nursery by now, little Hamlet and Polonius and Gertrude—"

"Claire," said Symonton, a tremble in his voice that did not sound like anger but more like a man caught somewhere between laughter and despair.

"Well, perhaps not Polonius, but you would have a nursery and family responsibilities and if that were the case, I would be the most recent London scandal and still be in search of a proper tutor for my brothers. I simply cannot be sorry about something that happened twelve years ago when it has made my life easier. There, I've said it and you may berate me for being self-serving and insensitive. I'm sure I deserve the scold." Her words had their desired effect for his mouth had turned into a full-blown grin and his eyes were alight with laughter.

"You do deserve something for your lamentable inability to recognize tragedy," Symonton retorted. By then they had pulled up in front of her house, the ride over. He was loath to see her go and thought he detected a similar feeling in her, but that might have been pure wishful thinking on his part. He searched for something to say to hold onto her company a moment longer and settled on, "Now about the prize you promised for finding a suitable tutor."

"*You* promised it on my behalf," Claire retorted, "but please continue. No doubt you deserve something for such exemplary and resolute service."

Symonton judged the moment right for offering her an initial but light-hearted hint of his affection, but at that moment the front door opened and the twins rushed outside.

"I say, your lordship, what a splendid pair!" Matt exclaimed in awe and before Symonton knew it, Claire murmured a thank you, took the groom's outstretched hand, and stepped down, leaving Symonton alone with her brothers. He didn't mind so very much. The boys were fresh and unspoiled in their admiration, and they were Claire's brothers, after all, but he thought the sun still dimmed a bit when the door closed behind her and knew with resigned certainty that it would always be so.

Claire met Mr. Freeman early the following week. She liked him immediately, with his open face and honest, attentive gaze behind small spectacles. She could see what it was about him that had allowed him to teach four sons without flinching. He gave the impression of unruffled practicality, every answer to her questions measured and sensible but without a hint of pomposity or prosing. That would have driven her brothers crazy, and herself as well. She was as bad as the boys when it came to being lectured.

"Lord Symonton tells me you are a pugilist of some reputation, Mr. Freeman," Claire remarked. It was hard to miss the large hands, muscled arms, and general athletic look of the man, so at odds with his educated speech and calm mannerisms.

"His lordship is too generous with his praise," Freeman responded. "I've seen Lord Symonton in the ring, and I don't pretend to that kind of skill and power."

"Lord Symonton?" Claire repeated blankly. "I had no idea."

"I hope I haven't been indiscreet, but it's well known at his club and through town that Symonton sets the form that the rest of us try to follow."

Claire found the contrast between the weary, bored Symonton she was used to and the Symonton who was admired for any kind of physical prowess too great to absorb just then. Of course, he was excellent with the reins, and he sat a horse very well, and he did have a more than acceptable physique. At one time she had noted with passing approval that he did not need the assistance of those outlandish stuffed coats that some of the younger dandies affected to improve their figures, as if people weren't bright enough to see that it was all padding and posturing. The mental picture of Symonton shirtless in the ring so engrossed her that she allowed a longer than comfortable silence in the room. Coming back to Mr. Freeman with a start, she apologized and asked about the cane he carried.

"It has nothing to do with any sportsman conduct, I'm afraid," he admitted cheerfully. "At the risk of making myself appear foolish and incompetent, I got up in the night and ran into a chair with my right foot and broke three toes. I hated owning up to it because I knew I'd take no end of teasing about it, and I was exactly right. The doctor says another two weeks and I can discard the cane and be back to my relatively sure-footed self."

After working out the details of the arrangement that included Claire's expectations for her brothers and Mr. Freeman's recommendations, the timing of his arrival in Sussex, and his living arrangements and wages once there, Claire rose to extend a hand.

"We will send a coach to get you from the Stanhopes. I feel the recipient of a great good fortune and hope you will enjoy your stay with us as much as you have your past years with Lord Stanhope."

"Lord Symonton spoke glowingly of you and your family, Lady Claire," Mr. Freeman replied, "and I don't take any recommendation he gives lightly because he gives them so rarely. Of course, there are the glories of the Sussex countryside as well. I'm sorry I can't meet the young viscount and his brother, but I'll plan on doing that the day of my arrival."

Claire had been frustrated at her inability to track down her brothers that particular morning. She had told them of Mr. Freeman's expected arrival and while not commanding their presence had hoped they would be curious enough to stand by in case she made an offer to him for his services. When she decided Mr. Freeman would do perfectly, Claire asked Crayton to find Matthew and William, but Crayton had to admit defeat. The two young men were nowhere to be found.

The boys were nearer than anyone thought, however—at the top of the stairs pressed against the wall, watchful and quiet. They had missed Mr. Freeman's arrival, but they caught a glimpse of him as he departed. Visible only from the back as Freeman walked beside Claire down the hallway to the front door, Matthew especially saw enough to strike despair into his youthful heart. The man seemed to be everything he dreaded, a tall, bent figure with a limp and leaning on a cane, too old and decrepit even to walk upright.

William looked at his brother quickly to see an expression of mute anger and desolation on Matt's face. *How could Claire do this to us?* was Matthew's silent question and all William could do was shrug in response. Twins inside and out, at that moment the two young minds thought as one.

Chapter 8

*T*he Penwarrens were packed and on their way to Loden Valley the last Monday in May, everyone except the twins glad to be going home. If it hadn't been for the looming threat of the tutor, the twins would have felt the same happy anticipation as their companions. As it was, the boys bid a despondent farewell to freedom.

"Quite the experience," remarked Mrs. Feastwell. She considered that she would have stories enough to last a lifetime. Who'd have thought the streets of London would be as nasty as they were? They made the countryside seem positively immaculate. At least at Loden Hall they knew what to do with the detritus of living, and it wasn't dump it out a window and hope no passerby was splattered.

Moira settled back comfortably in the seat thinking much the same. There had been that greengrocer's boy that tried to convince her to stay in London, but Moira was no fool. She had a good situation with the Penwarrens, fair loved Miss Claire, and she was not about to throw it all away for some fresh-faced young fellow with only one thing on his mind. Moira's mother had married young and what did she have to show but ten children and a two-room hut, never enough on the table despite the baskets of food Miss Claire insisted on sending home with Moira, and hands that cracked every winter from the cold. Now that she'd experienced life with the Penwarrens, Moira had no intention of doing anything but serving Miss Claire her whole life. It would suit her just fine.

Mrs. Crayton, feeling her lumbago, rearranged her posture and simply enjoyed the warm ride home.

Once at Loden Hall, Claire picked up where she had left off. There was a stack of finished bed and window coverings from the local seamstress waiting for her, and she expected several pieces of furniture she had selected and purchased in London to arrive that very week. Most of the linens had been counted and cleaned and the kitchen scrubbed to gleaming with new pots and pans hanging from the ceiling. The satisfaction of planning, organizing, and supervising was what Claire needed right now.

Harry Macapee's delight in Cecelia's company, already of enormous proportion, had increased with the satisfactory disappearance of The Honourable Charles Hustisford. Cecelia was serenely happy with Harry, as well, and it was clear to Claire that barring her father's complete disapproval, which was unlikely, she would soon lose her sister to a husband. Since her father found it impossible to deny his children anything and since Harry Macapee was a young man of good countenance and good family with a respectable future in the army, Claire thought the marriage would occur sooner rather than later. She had mixed feelings about the nuptials, most of them rooted unbecomingly in self-interest, but outwardly refused to do anything but rejoice for her sister. Sometimes at night, though, when she thought of Cecelia's room empty and the sister she loved and had defended all her life hundreds of miles away, Claire could almost have wept—if she were the weeping type, which she certainly wasn't.

The twins, especially Matthew, were sullen and quiet even before departing London, lost their boisterous good humor and their inveterate interest in all things mischievous, and once home did not even bother to seek out Betcher in the stables. If Claire had not been rushing about ordering last minute household items to be shipped from London as well as organizing the family's departure, she would have set aside a morning with her brothers to get to the bottom of their bad humor. She did not find the time, however, and told herself she would get to it when they were settled once again at Loden Hall and she had finished refurbishing her father's bedchamber. Her sisterly guess was that the boys were disappointed to leave the attractions of the big city and had decided to pout a little to show their displeasure. Such behavior seemed unlike them, but they were growing up and changing, and she knew that sometimes children's growing pains were as much in their heads and hearts as in their bodies. She would share the details about Mr. Freeman when they got home and believed the twins would be pleased with her selection. They worshipped Symonton, so the fact that he recommended Freeman would hold great weight, and just the idea that their tutor could instruct in the basics of fist fighting would go a long way in appeasing Matt's dislike for the idea of formal and regular instruction.

Their penultimate day in London was a trying one for Claire. She had a hundred things to do and was occupied making a list of their order of importance when Moira brought word that Sir Walter was in the drawing room and insisted on an audience with Miss Claire. Claire headed downstairs in a small temper she would not let show, only to have her cousin fall on one knee before her and beg her hand in marriage as soon as she entered the room and closed the door behind her. Claire was aghast at his action and more irritated than flattered, but she tried to be as kind as her impatience would allow.

"Sir Walter—cousin—please stand up. Really, you needn't cause yourself such discomfort. I'm convinced that such a posture cannot be good for one's knees and I wouldn't have you injure yourself." He tried to grab one of Claire's hands in his as he rose, but she hastily stepped back and purposefully clasped both her hands behind her back.

"My deep fondness cannot come as a surprise to you, dear cousin Claire. Surely you have remarked on my attention these past weeks and noted the pleasure I find in your company. It was the becoming modesty of your responses to my small gestures of affection that first convinced me of your reciprocal attraction." Claire was somewhere between horror and exasperation.

"Sir Walter, you do me an honor I cannot properly articulate"—at least that part was true—"but I must refuse your offer. My first loyalty is to my family and I must always put their needs above mine."

"That is just the type of response I have come to expect from you," Thatcher replied with smug approval. "Your faithfulness does you credit, cousin, but your siblings need not be such a burden for you. You have a father, after all, and he should not expect a tender girl such as yourself to carry out what are rightfully his responsibilities. But it would not be fitting for me to say more on that point out of your father's presence." Thatcher added the last sentence hastily, having seen a light come into Claire's eyes that brought unbidden imaginations of the heat of battle. Had Napoleon confronted a similar expression on the face of the Iron Duke?

"Certainly your sister could return to her own people"—Thatcher imbued the last three words with a patronizing distaste that raised the hairs on the back of Claire's neck—"and there are several fine schools that will take boys of your brothers' age."

Sometime during his speech Moira, with the perfect intuition of the finest ladies' maids, opened the doors to the drawing room and patiently, strategically waited for Thatcher to pause for breath before announcing softly, "Here's Lord Symonton, Miss."

Symonton stood in the doorway for only a moment before coming forward. Any pea brain could interpret the situation, Claire's face a study in flaming annoyance and her body backing away from Thatcher as if he brandished a weapon and was attempting to steal the family's silver.

Thatcher turned to Symonton saying with unconcealed outrage, "I say, Symonton, this is a private conversation," to which Claire responded, relief at Symonton's arrival evident on her face and in her voice, "No, Sir Walter, our conversation here is done. I have given you my answer and it will not change."

Thatcher glared at Symonton, waiting for his lordship to apologize and tactfully back out of the room, but Symonton, reading Claire's expression correctly, entered the room instead and made himself comfortable in the chair closest to the couple.

"I'm afraid I have important business to discuss with Lady Claire, Thatcher," Symonton murmured, pulling off his gloves with fastidious deliberation. "Do you think you could finish your conversation within the hour? I'll wait." Gloves removed, he crossed his legs with casual elegance and gave a vague smile, a man of exquisite long-suffering prepared to wait the entire concluding hour for his own audience with Claire.

Claire took Thatcher's arm in a firm grip. "An hour would be completely unnecessary because Sir Walter and I are quite finished, Symonton, and I'm sure you must be here about the plumbing."

"Indeed. Yes. The plumbing it is," Symonton agreed without blink or pause.

Claire pulled Thatcher along to the door where Moira waited.

"So kind of you, cousin. Such an honor. Words fail me. Now here's Moira with your hat and I must bid you good bye. So much to do, you know, as we prepare for our return trip to Sussex and there is that pesky plumbing problem to deal with. Be assured that meeting you was an unexpected addition to the season for which I cannot find adequate or suitable words."

Moira, holding the outside door open as Claire gently shoved Thatcher out onto the step, just as gently pulled the door shut behind him. Claire leaned against the back of the door for a moment and met Moira's innocent look.

"Will there be anything else, Miss?" the girl asked. Claire straightened.

"No, Moira. Thank-you." They both understood the heartfelt feeling behind the last two words. Symonton rose when Claire reentered the drawing room.

"Plumbing, Claire?" he drawled, giving her a reproachful look.

"Oh, do be quiet, Symonton," she said crossly, but a smile was slowly reappearing in her eyes. "It's not easy to think of excuses when one has just received an unwelcome offer from a man who had the temerity to suggest I send my sister back to her own people—as if *we* weren't exactly that—and my brothers away to school so we needn't be bothered by the demands of family." She gave her head a little shake to clear it of those offensive suggestions. "Anyway, thank-you for your timely appearance. Are you here for some specific purpose or just to rescue me yet again from my own bad humor?"

"I won't take up your time," he said. It was clear her mind was on a hundred things other than him. "I know you leave tomorrow and I just wanted to wish you an uneventful trip. I plan to accompany my sister to Sussex at the end of the week and then I'm off to Cornwall for the summer." His words brought Claire up short.

"The whole summer, Symonton?" She couldn't have said why she felt that sudden and sharp dismay, that sinking feeling in her stomach, but there it was. "Who will I call on if I have the unattractive urge to shriek like a fishwife?"

"I'm afraid you'll have to shriek away and suffer the consequences on your own, Claire, unless you think you can reach a volume level that will carry across counties and drown out the ocean."

"I'm talented but I fear not that talented." Claire remembered to smile again. "I wish you a good trip and a productive summer, but—strictly for friendship's sake, Symonton—I encourage you to brighten Symonton Manor while you're there. A whole summer in the midst of everything dark and plain would not improve your—how did you put it?—bleak temperament."

She had mentally adjusted now to the idea of his extended absence and was a little ashamed of herself for that quick feeling of abandonment she'd experienced. She must remember they were just friends and relatively new friends, at that. He certainly had a life and other interests beyond the Penwarrens. To compensate for her lowered spirits, Claire spoke with more cheer than she felt.

"I can understand that you may not wish to improve it, of course. While I've never seen the attraction, Lord Byron made a bleak temperament fashionably romantic and perhaps you feel you must cultivate the pretense to impress your friends, though I warn you that romantic moping grows old quickly, especially for the people who must observe it on a regular basis." She smiled to ensure he understood she was teasing and added more soberly, "I hope you will be able to come by Loden Hall before you leave, Symon, since Mr. Freeman is arriving early in the week. I think he would welcome kind words from you before he commences with what I'm convinced is going to be a more challenging task in tandem than the Stanhopes ever were in quartet."

Claire did not walk in beauty as the night, Symonton mused, his mind distracted by the thought of Byron. She was more daytime, sunlight, blue skies, and rolling green hills, with nothing hidden or mysterious about her, every dear thought readable on her face, every laugh making its first appearance in her eyes. Byron could have been referring to Claire there at the end, though: *The smiles that win, the tints that glow / But tell of days in goodness spent / A mind at peace with all below / A heart whose love is innocent.* Or if not innocent, at least distracted and preoccupied, which were no good to any suit he might wish to bring. He responded to the tone of her last comment.

"The boys are still causing problems?"

A little vertical crease between her brows that he'd come to recognize as a sign of worry appeared.

"Something's afoot, and I think I'm likely doing them and me a disservice by not addressing it right now, but there's so much to be done that I can't seem to find a minute, and when I do, I can't find the boys."

Symonton stood, saying kindly, "Don't let it trouble you too much. They're boys, after all, and as easily moved from admiring my livestock to chasing ducks in the park. Once you're home they'll be more themselves."

"What a good friend you are to care about my ragamuffin bunch!" She spoke with heartfelt warmth and to detract a little from what she thought he might consider an unattractive fervor in her tone added with a playful look, "Regardless of what people say, you are no Ice Man to us."

He thought it might be just the moment to say that she had become much more than a friend to him, that he found days without her dragging and tedious, that his nights were filled with tantalizing images of her responding to his attentions with the focused passion he'd glimpsed the night of the Steppingtons' ball, that he thought about her nearly constantly, pictured her beside him, heard her laugh when she was nowhere near, and was altogether and completely, hopelessly besotted with her. God, that it had come to this! He was a fool, but he could no more cease thinking about Claire Penwarren than he could stop breathing.

Symonton would not say any of that, of course. It was hardly the moment for it, but perhaps he could give a hint, just a hint, of his feelings, something for her to ponder during the months they would be apart.

"Claire," he began but the doors opened and Sophie stepped inside.

"Oh, it's you, Symonton," the woman said by way of greeting, then turned to Claire. "Can you come, Claire? There's a delivery man wanting to deliver a large bureau at the back door. Didn't you mean for it to go to Sussex?"

"Oh, bother, of course I did! What would we do with it here, drag it home behind the coach? I thought that man would get it wrong, no matter how clearly I explained what I wanted. Tell him I'll be there directly." She turned to Symonton and put out a hand. "I must go. Thank you for your timely appearance today and will you promise not to leave for Cornwall without saying goodbye?"

He took her hand, a touch at least and more than he had expected so he would be, must be, happy with that for the time being.

"I promise."

Then she was gone and he found his own way out.

For Claire, the ungainly and unwelcome proposal from Walter Thatcher had been unpleasant, but the news that Symonton would be gone the whole summer and perhaps into the fall had produced in her a real, deep, and surprising unhappiness. She was glad when that particular day was over and they were finally on their way to Sussex, gladder still when she could see the hall's solid outline in the distance. How had she ever thought the place gloomy and dismal? It was home now.

The week scheduled for Mr. Freeman's arrival started out gray, wet, and unseasonably cool. Claire put the finishing touches on her father's chambers, done in his favorite colors of cinnamon and cream, rich and warm and comfortable just the way he liked it, just like her father, in fact. A rich, warm, and comfortable man. They had all learned to love color during the years they spent in India, wonderful rich tones that lifted the spirits, nothing like the tasteful neutral drabs that Claire had seen so much of since her arrival. The day disappeared as she worked, supervising everything from the placement of furniture to the pictures hanging on the walls.

She wanted Mr. Freeman to be comfortable, too, and there was the schoolroom to be polished and outfitted. Claire was not especially competitive by nature, but she was determined not to come off shabby next to the Stanhopes. She had been up early as usual and waved away any thought of luncheon. The sky was dim, but the June day still offered some light and Claire was determined to finish one or two more tasks when Sophie appeared in the doorway. Claire had been barely conscious of the light drizzle that had begun earlier in the afternoon, but with Sophie's appearance she heard heavy raindrops beating against the windows. The increasing storm abruptly erased the last vestiges of June daylight and wind gusts made the roof creak.

"Come to supper, Claire," Sophie directed. "You've been like a dervish all day, and the rest of us are getting hungry waiting for you. I've put a fire in the dining room, and we can have a cozy meal. Bring the boys, too."

Claire searched for her brothers without success and finally returned to the dining room where Cecelia and Sophie waited.

"I thought Matt and Will would be down here because they're nowhere upstairs." She came in as far as the table, noted the two empty chairs, and added, "How odd that they aren't here! Wherever could they have gotten to?"

As she spoke William slid into the room behind her and took his seat at the table, his thin, sensitive face pale and expressionless, his eyes downcast.

"Will, is Matt behind you?" asked Claire. "I can't scold for being late when I'm just getting here myself." The boy didn't answer, only raised his head to meet Claire's gaze.

She caught the uncertainty and mute unhappiness there and abruptly sat down next to him, saying kindly, "What is it?" Something about his look caused an alarm to begin ringing softly in her head and her heartbeat to pick up speed. "Is Matt coming?"

Will shook his head slightly. "No."

"Where is he, then?" It was clear Will was torn between loyalty to Matt, concern for his brother's well being, and love for his sister. The boy's face was a picture of misery.

Cecelia, sitting on the other side of William, reached to put a hand on his arm. "What is it, Will?"

It was her gentle question that brought the response. "He's gone."

"Gone?" Claire repeated the word as if it were a Russian syllable she had never heard before. "How can he be gone?"

"He packed a few things and left. He said he wasn't going to spend the rest of his life in a schoolroom with a stuffy old man learning about a lot of nonsense he'd never use in his life."

"Left?" Claire felt she had been reduced to repeating single-syllable words, but nothing else seemed to be making sense and she seemed incapable of stringing words together into coherent sentences. Outside the wind picked up even more and they could hear rain drumming against the roof.

It was Cecelia who asked the sensible questions, her tone conversational and gently inquiring. "Where did Matt go?"

"I don't know. He wouldn't say. He made me promise not to tell anyone. I had to swear on our blood as brothers and now I've broken my word." His voice sounded very young and cracked with the final phrase.

"It doesn't count if the oath was a bad one to start with," Claire declared simply, finally regaining some of her faculties. "When did Matt leave?"

"This morning."

Morning, Claire thought with a sinking heart, while I was enraptured with portraits and carpets. She had meant all along to spend time with her brothers, as soon as she finished the rooms upstairs, at some undesignated time but soon, she had told herself. She would tell them about Mr. Freeman's prowess and how he came recommended by Symonton. And if only she had done so, if only she had put people ahead of things, the information would have raised the tutor enough in her brothers' estimation to avoid this terrible moment. She had meant to—oh, she truly had!—but with so many things to do, she never found or took the time, always planning for tomorrow. Now all she could see was the empty chair across the table and a tomorrow, a string of tomorrows, without Matt. There was a momentary quiet in the room, everyone wordlessly listening to the storm pounding against the house, everyone picturing one small boy out in it. Then Claire rose briskly, despair and despondency banished, plans to be set in motion, work to be done.

"I'll go to Betcher and see if he knows anything about Matt's intentions. Cece, you ask Crayton and Moira—she doesn't miss much—and any of the other servants in the house the same. Aunt Sophie, would you please find Mrs. Feastwell and see if Matt stopped in the kitchen to take a meal with him? He's very practical about his appetite." The two women rose and started out immediately, Claire, too, until she stopped and looked back at William, a small and forlorn figure sitting alone at the big table. She went back to him to pull him up and gather him into her arms, an eleven-year-old boy temporarily going on three. "It will be all right, Will. I know you didn't know what to do."

William loved his sister Claire, loved her good sense and the way she never talked down to him and his brother or treated them as if they weren't grown and sensible boys, loved the smell of her, too, a touch of rosewater that had comforted him since he could remember.

"I came to find you," he said, his voice muffled against her, "and tell you, or at least ask you what to do. I had planned how I could do it without breaking my promise to Matt, but you were busy with everything, putting up the curtains and such, and I didn't think I should bother you."

His words hurt her more than even the Steppingtons' comments had. One dear brother thought he could not bother her, and the other thought he must run away from her. Run away from the very one he should have been able to run to. Her heart felt ragged and torn.

"It will be all right," she repeated and kissed him lightly on the top of his head. "Why don't you go look in Matt's room to see if he left anything behind as a clue to his whereabouts?"

With everyone assigned their duties, Claire threw a heavy cape around her shoulders, pulled up the hood, and braved her way to the stables. If it had not been storming there would still have been late light in the summer day, but the rain clouds made it seem like night.

"I seen the lad this morning," said Betcher. "He was asking about Bristol and how far it was, how long it would take to get there and such. Asked if I thought a boy his size could stow away on a ship without being caught. I thought he was just being a boy, thinking about great adventures as boys do." Betcher's troubled expression said he suddenly realized Matt hadn't been playing at sailor.

The air was cold but Claire went colder. Headed for Bristol on foot in the middle of this storm! How far could he have gotten? Would he have taken the main road or tried to elude pursuit by going across country? Would he be able to stay on course or eventually just wander aimlessly across the Sussex countryside? How would one even attempt to find him?

"Betcher, I need you to ride to Lord Symonton, who I hope has arrived at his sister's by now. Tell him what's happened and that I need to ask his advice. Have something saddled for me before you leave. I must change to riding clothes."

"Miss, you can't go out in this storm."

"Yes, I can," Claire retorted grimly. "Do you think I would allow my brother to be out alone in this dark weather and not go in search of him?" and she was gone, half-running back to the house to throw on a heavy riding suit and find a dry cape.

Symonton and Lady Pasturson had arrived back in Sussex one day earlier. Harry came with them, too, but dined at the big hall with his brother that night; it was just Symonton and his sister in the Dower House. They had finished supper and were seated comfortably by the fire sipping claret with no need to make conversation. Margaret had tried, but Symonton was uncharacteristically quiet and thoughtful.

"Must you leave for Cornwall now, Robert? There's the church fete and the squire's annual outdoor gala next week."

"As hard as it is to resist such exuberant decadence, yes, I must leave now. It's been months since I've been to Symonton, and I'm past due."

"But later would do just as well. Since the Penwarrens are back, it might not be so deadly dull for you here. I sometimes think you are quite in charity with Lady Claire."

It was the most she had ever dared to say about her brother's private feelings, and he raised his eyes to hers. For a moment she saw a startling flash of emotion there, then it was gone and he said easily, "Only when she is not condemning me for my self-indulgence. Her scolds do not leave me feeling charitable about her at all." He turned his attention back to the fire, and the room was quiet until the simultaneous ringing of the bell and pounding on the door.

As soon as Betcher's voice sounded at the opened door, Symonton was up on his feet and out into the hallway, Margaret on his heels. He heard the story of Matt's flight and was bounding up the stairs to change even before Betcher had finished speaking.

"Tell Patterson to saddle Bonaparte for my brother," Margaret directed Betcher calmly. "He won't be but a minute." Symonton was back in even less time, covered with a greatcoat. "You'll get soaked," Margaret fretted but he didn't bother to respond. It was clear to her that the words *Miss Claire needs you* drove any other thoughts from Symonton's head, and she felt a warm and strong affection for him just then. She had hoped someday he would love, and it was clear to her now that he did, completely, irrevocably, and apparently forever. She could only hope, for all their sakes, that such potent feeling was reciprocated or her brother would be unbearable and they would all suffer for years to come.

Symonton met Claire in the middle of the road that led from the Dower House to Loden Hall. The rain had abated a great deal, clouds scudded away with the quick, cool wind, and pale late daylight began to assert itself. The quick summer storm seemed to be over.

"Go home, Claire," his lordship directed. "I'll gather some men and lanterns. Matthew can't have gotten all that far."

Her colorless, stricken face was resolute. "He's been gone all day. I can't sit at home and do nothing when he's out in this dark, wet night. I should have paid more attention to him, Symon, but I was too busy. Now look."

"You are developing a martyr-like attitude that is as boring as it is unflattering," Symonton replied coolly. "Now go home and let me handle this. It would do no good for me to have to worry about you along with your bothersome brother." She sent him a quick look that shifted instantaneously from annoyed to grateful.

"Of course, you're right. Aren't you always?" He was glad to detect a hint of irony in her tone. "I'm sorry if I seem embarrassingly self-indulgent. I'll have Betcher join you with our stable boys. Did he tell you Matt was headed for Bristol?"

"Yes. Stowing away held some attraction for me when I was his age, too."

"Really? I can't picture it. You'd have been out on deck directing captain and crew in your usual peremptory manner before you even left port." Her weak attempt at light-heartedness touched him more than anything else she could have said.

"Go home, Claire," he repeated more gently, "and leave my officious and arrogant childhood out of the discussion." She turned without further comment toward home.

It was Symonton that found Matt several hours later. They had searched as much as they could before night made it impossible, a dark night with mounds of clouds blowing across and often obscuring the moon, and Symonton eventually sent everyone home. He was pleased that both his nephews had come out, and when Symonton finally declared that the search was doing no good and would resume in the morning, Vernon had headed to his home and Harry had gone in the direction of Loden Hall. It was a foregone conclusion that his nephew would marry Cecelia. The boy said her name like a prayer and could seem to speak about nothing and no one else. Had Symonton not found himself in a similar situation, he'd have teased his nephew unmercifully. As it was, he felt sympathy for such painful love sickness. It was everything and more, both better and worse, than he could have imagined—if he'd ever spent any time thinking about the malady, that is, which until the intrusion of Claire Penwarren into his life he'd never had a need or desire to do.

Symonton could not bring himself to go back to Loden Hall and see the look on Claire's face when he admitted failure. The only thing worse would be taking her bad news. He thought he would go just a little farther west, just a few more miles, one more stream, one more hill, just one small village farther, with his hope of success dwindling with each mile. So when he crested the hill, he thought at first that the figure was a trick of moonlight and shadows. There was a stream, running full and fast from the torrential rain, and a figure lying half in the water and half on the bank. A large rock, he had thought at first, or a bundle of old clothes but as he went closer, his throat constricted so tightly he couldn't have called out even if he'd wanted to. There were several rocks at that particular location that would have suited as stepping stones to cross the stream, but with the sudden influx of rainwater those stones would have been submerged, slippery, and treacherous. Symonton, crouching by an unconscious Matt, thought that was what had happened. The boy had tried to cross the stream and lost his balance on the very first stone. Symonton said an uncharacteristic prayer of thanks, for if Matt had fallen mid-stream and knocked himself unconscious, he might have drowned. Symonton could not imagine anything worse than having to tell that to Claire, didn't think he could have borne the grief and the guilt he would have seen in her eyes. At least the boy was breathing. Matt had a large bruise and bump on his head, and from the unnatural bend of his arm, Symonton guessed the bone was broken, but still, still, the boy was alive.

It was early morning hours when he rode into the yard of Loden Hall carrying his precious burden, but all the windows in the place remained lit. Betcher came to the door of the stables and for a moment didn't know what to do first—run toward his lordship or up to the house. He chose the latter.

Claire was up and still dressed for riding, but she had shed her jacket to reveal a high-necked white shirt beneath. She emerged from the front door and ran ahead of Betcher and his lantern, coming up to Symonton as he sat Bonaparte with Matt propped against his chest and encircled by his arms. Claire's face was ashen, frozen; only her eyes were alive and pleading.

"Oh, Symonton, he's not—" Her gaze fixed on the limp body of her brother, his coat tied tightly around his chest in an odd configuration she would later realize was his lordship's clever way of keeping Matt's arm immobile. At the time, however, stricken by fear, she fixed only on Matt's waxen face and could not bring herself to finish the sentence.

"No, no," Symonton said quickly. "He's had a hard knock to the head and I think his left arm is broken, but he's alive. He stirred more than once on the ride home and even awoke long enough to ask for you."

With a warning to watch Matt's arm, Symonton handed him down to Betcher and as heavy as the boy was, Claire demanded him. Once Matt was safely, tenderly transferred to her embrace, she buried her face for a moment against the boy's neck.

Finally she raised her head, that terrible, frozen expression gone, her voice once more calm and practical, and said, "Go immediately for the doctor, Betcher. Roust him out and bring him at once." She turned with her brother in her arms toward the house where Harry had come forward to assist with the weight of Claire's welcome burden. With Harry beside her, Claire halted long enough to look back at Symonton, who sat wet and weary.

"My lord, you're soaked. Come in by the fire and have something hot." With only the slightest crack to her voice revealing her emotion she added, "I can never thank you for this. Never. There aren't words." Then they were up the steps and in the front door, Cecelia and Sophie and young Will first standing just inside and then crowding forward as Moira closed the door behind them all.

Just a moment ago, Symonton had been cold and tired, as extreme in both as he could ever remember being. But seeing the light return to Claire's face and hearing the joy in her voice caused all the chill and weariness to drop away. He was refreshed and energized, ready to embark on another quest if that was what it took to keep Claire happy.

Later Symonton and young William sat in front of the fire in the library, the boy stiff and unmoving until Symonton had pity on him.

"Your brother will be fine, William," he told him quietly. "He'll have a bruise that will be the envy of the neighborhood and he won't be able to use his left arm for a few weeks, but that will all pass and he'll be right as rain."

"I didn't know what to do," Will shared in a small voice. "I promised on my honor not to tell but it got to raining and Claire was so stern—" His voice trickled off.

"Sometimes a man must make hard decisions," Symonton said. He could not think of many hard decisions he'd had to make in his privileged years, but he supposed, if he ever got his heart's desire, that as a husband and a father he might have to do so. Privately, he thought Claire would be much better at hard decisions than he but all he wanted to do at the moment was comfort William.

"One considers all the possibilities, weighs the right and wrong of things, makes the decision, and sticks by it." William was watching Symonton's face avidly and listening to every word. "Isn't that what you did?"

The boy nodded.

"Then you have nothing to be ashamed of. In fact, it's very likely you helped save your brother's life. What if you hadn't said anything and Matthew had lain all night in the cold and the wet? There's no telling what might have happened. You made a decision and it was the right one. Matthew will understand and your father will be proud of you." It was apparently the right thing to say, for William snuggled back in the big chair and the next time Symonton looked over at him the boy was soundly asleep.

Later, after the doctor came and went, Sophie stopped to tell Symonton the welcome news that Matt seemed to have sustained no lasting damage, just the bump on his head and the broken arm as Symonton had guessed.

"We're all very grateful to you," the woman told him with gruff emotion. He waved a hand nonchalantly in the air.

"Pure chance that I found him. I was happy to help."

"I'm sure you were," said Sophie with a look on her face half amused, half serious. If his lordship wanted to take this indifferent attitude when it had been clear to her for weeks that he was completely smitten with her elder niece, she would humor him. "Claire asked me to send you home. She said she'll be up with the boy all night and asked if you could find time to stop by tomorrow."

He felt a small regret that he wouldn't see Claire again that night—that morning, really—but said, "Of course. I was just staying long enough to hear the doctor's report."

Sophie refrained from an unladylike snort. From Symonton's reaction to her words, it was clear as day he'd been hanging around to catch another glimpse of Claire. Then she softened. She'd been head over heels once, too, but her parents had nipped that soon enough. Thomas, Lord Loden, had come angling, and he was a better catch than Sophie's desire, a cleric of no title and modest means. So she had told her young man good-bye and spent the next thirty years in misery and regret. She wouldn't wish that on anyone, and if Claire had an affection for this lofty, cool-eyed man, she'd wish them both happy and dance at their wedding. All that remained to be seen, of course, but after tonight she thought the nuptials just might take place.

Harry departed to share the good news with his brother and his mother, and it was Cecelia returning from their fond good night that discovered the sleeping William. She put him to bed before she came into Matt's room where Claire sat.

"Claire, the doctor gave Matt something to make him sleep. He won't waken before mid-morning. Go to bed. I can sit with him for a while." Claire raised her gaze to her sister.

"I can't sleep, Cece, so it's just as well I stay here. Despite the draft the doctor prescribed, Matt's still restless and even if he doesn't know I'm here, it makes me feel better to sit with him."

"We have a good friend in Symonton," Cecelia remarked simply as she headed out of Matt's room on her way to bed.

Claire could still see his lordship soaked and tired atop that great horse with Matt in his arms. She remembered her first despairing thought at the sight. Her brother had looked so little and limp her heart had actually stopped a moment thinking Symonton held a lifeless body. Then Symonton's eyes had met hers, quick to assure her even without words that everything was all right, and her organs had started up again, heart pumping, blood running through her veins, brain once more functioning.

She looked at Matt against the pillow, freckles showing brown against his pale face and a purple bruise continuing to spread over his eye, but alive, warm and safe and home where he belonged.

"Yes," Claire said finally, "a very good friend."

Chapter 9

Claire took some sleep soon after sunrise when Sophie came in and scooted her out, and she awoke after a few hours refreshed and invigorated. Matt had slept well through the night and the sun shone brilliantly through the windows. Everything portended a day much happier than the day before. She replaced her aunt on the chair next to her brother's bed and was just settling her skirts when the boy awoke. Matt looked around the room, confused and somewhat panicked, saw Claire, and croaked out her name. She was at his side in a moment, kneeling next to the bed and stroking back his hair. She watched memory catch up with his eyes.

"I'm sorry," he said finally.

"You should be sorry," Claire responded, but lovingly. "We all worried ourselves sick about you. I'm sorry, too, Matt. I should have been more interested in you than furniture and linens, but I wasn't. I'll forgive you if you will forgive me." At his affectionate nod, she leaned to kiss him.

"I remember trying to cross a stream. I must have slipped."

"Yes, that's what Lord Symonton said he thought happened. He found you and brought you home."

"How?" He stared at Claire and recognized the message of her smile. "On Bonaparte? Did his lordship bring me home on Bonaparte, Claire?" Her brother had admired that animal from first sight.

"Yes."

"Wouldn't you know?" the boy asked in disgust. "Wouldn't you just know? And I can't even remember it."

"Perhaps you'll get another chance," Claire said, but thought with a pang of loss that it would not be for some months. Symonton was scheduled to leave this week and would not return until late autumn. The summer stretched endlessly. She had to change the subject if she didn't want to slide into an immediate depression at the prospect of the Symonton-less months ahead.

"You'll have to concentrate on mending your arm, Matt. Symonton tells me that Mr. Freeman is quite the pugilist. You'll want to learn more than proper stance, I'm sure, but until your arm is completely healed, you'll have to settle for that." All she needed to complete the day's happiness was to see Matt's bright smile at the unexpected information about his new tutor.

He soon grew sleepy again but managed to murmur, "I really am sorry, Claire. I wasn't exactly running away. More like running toward." Then he was asleep once more.

Claire kept herself busy with needlework for the morning until Cecelia came in.

"Let me sit a while, Claire. Lord Symonton's been waiting patiently downstairs for you for at least a quarter hour."

"But no one told me!" Claire cried and let her embroidery fall to the floor without a second thought as she quickly stood. "I wouldn't have kept him waiting, of all people."

"Will was quizzing him about Mr. Freeman until Aunt Sophie called Will away to luncheon, so his lordship hasn't been cooling his heels all that long."

Claire didn't stay long enough to hear the details. She was down the stairs and into the drawing room by the time Cecelia finished speaking. Symonton, standing by the mantel with his hands in his pockets when Claire rushed in, gave her a careful look. Eyes a little tired, perhaps, but otherwise none the worse for last night. In fact, dressed in that yellow muslin dress with small green fronds embroidered around the hem and sleeves, she looked like sunshine personified. Claire stopped abruptly just inside the door.

"Symon," she said, a world of warmth and some other, more profound emotion coloring her voice.

Symonton, naturally and without foresight, opened his arms to her and Claire with the same effortless and instinctive movement came into his embrace and relaxed against his chest as if she belonged there, as if he were home to her. In the quiet Symonton thought it the perfect time to tell her of his feelings, tell her he loved her more than life and ask her if she thought she could possibly, some day, by some wild imagining, learn to love him in return. He said her name and paused for the most infinitesimal of moments—just to be sure he started the declaration off properly—when they were both aware of a commotion in the front hall. The drawing room doors were partly open and he could clearly hear a man's voice calling.

"Claire! Cecelia! Boys! Confound it, where are my children?" Claire pushed herself away and looked up at Symonton, delight in her eyes.

"Oh, Symon, it's Papa!" she cried and was out of his arms in an instant and into the hallway, laughing and crying and throwing herself into the embrace of the tall, robust man standing there.

Symonton, suddenly cold despite the June sunshine pouring in the front windows, bereft of the only thing he ever wanted to have in his arms again, came to the door to watch the family reunion—Cecelia flying down the staircase to throw herself at the newcomer with uncharacteristic zeal and Will leaping into the man's arms and clinging to his neck for dear life. Papa it is, thought Symonton ruefully, and if you'd planned your arrival an hour later, sir, there might have been a different greeting between us.

As it was, Claire drew Symonton forward, explaining his role in yesterday's incident. Lord Loden shook his hand heartily and expressed his thanks more than once before bounding up the steps to see his elder son.

Everyone followed in his wake but Claire stopped at the foot of the steps long enough to say shyly, "Can you stay for tea? It will be especially grand in Papa's honor."

Symonton shook his head. "No, I'm intruding." She said, "Never!" in protest as he added, "I'm off today for Cornwall, Claire. I only came by to see how your brother fared. My bags are packed and the horses hitched." He thought her face fell, but it may just have been wanting it to be so that gave the illusion.

"I wish you didn't have to go," was all Claire said. Neither spoke of that brief earlier moment when they had fit together so exactly right it was as if they had been made for each other.

"Seeing your father, I can tell you will have plenty to keep yourself busy."

"Yes, but—" She stopped herself at the last moment from saying "it won't be the same without you" and asked instead, "When will we see you again?"

"Late September, most likely, unless your sister and my nephew plan their nuptials sooner than that." Neither Symonton nor Claire anticipated any obstacle to the match from Loden.

"It will take me longer than three months to get Cecelia's wedding organized," Claire answered, laughing. "I have plans for it that people will talk about for years to come."

"Baskets of rose petals and ascending doves?"

She laughed again. "Something like that."

Then Cecelia came to the top of the steps to call her sister upstairs, and Claire gave Symonton one last small smile before she ascended to join the family in Matt's room.

Not long after, Symonton left, too, left Sussex for the windswept Cornish coast and thought he had not been too far from the truth when he said the place would fit his bleak temperament. Bleak was an apt description of his emotions as the miles that separated him from Claire increased.

With Lord Loden home, Claire finally felt able to relax. Matt's arm was healing fine, what she'd accomplished with the house pleased her father, and Aunt Sophie was to stay on indefinitely or forever, whichever came first. Mr. Freeman arrived and was slowly and wisely gaining the twins' trust. She couldn't remember being more content with family togetherness but discovered that being content was strangely unaligned with private happiness. For reasons she could not name, Claire felt fidgety and vaguely melancholic. That she should feel so unsettled was mystifying and slightly embarrassing. Any other time, having her family safely together under one roof would have set her singing through the house. That she did not feel one whit like singing annoyed her. She thought it must be Cecelia's engagement that caused the vague disquiet and did not allow herself to consider other explanations for her uneasy days and restless nights.

"Tell me about this Harry Macapee," her father said after one of his first suppers home and taking Claire's arm, the two strolled through the gardens, she talking and Loden listening. "Will he make Cece happy, do you think?"

Recalling the distress her own plan for Cecelia's happiness had caused, Claire answered humbly, "He loves her very much, Papa, and she him. He's intelligent and kind, with integrity and certainly of good family. It's only her future as a soldier's wife that concerns me."

Her father responded obliquely, "Well, we'll see about that."

Harry formally asked for Cecelia's hand on the twenty-first of June, summer solstice and the day after King William died. England went into mourning, but it was all far removed from the Sussex countryside and didn't much dim anyone's happiness. The old king had not been all that loved and the gay young queen, Victoria, now wore the crown. The country people liked the idea of a lass on the throne, Mrs. Feastwell going so far as to bake a cake in the new queen's honor, festooned with royal colors and live roses from the garden. Then she baked another cake in honor of Cecelia's and Harry's engagement. A wedding cake would be forthcoming in October. The kitchen hummed with happiness.

Claire accompanied her father when he paid his first visit to Harry's mother, Lady Pasturson.

"I know I should remember her," Loden told Claire, "but as I recall she came here with Pasturson the year your mother died, and it wasn't long after that Thomas took the title and you and I left for India. Sophie wrote about her now and then, but I confess I wouldn't be able to recognize her today."

Claire thought Lady Pasturson and her father got along very well from the first. They seemed to find plenty to talk about, mutual friends and shared memories, and both seemed happy with the match between their children. Claire had never noticed a resemblance between Harry and his mother before, but on more than one occasion over the summer she saw in Margaret the same kind face and intelligent eyes that Harry possessed. Something else, too—a glow of happiness, but Harry's glow could be credited to his love for Cecelia and Claire could not credit the same cause for Lady Pasturson's radiance. Perhaps it was only that summer warmth agreed with the older woman. Whatever the reason, she looked increasingly happy and spirited. Sometimes Claire would nonchalantly ask her neighbor about Symonton and Lady Pasturson would invariably respond with the same words, "He seems to be doing very well, Claire. Very well. Thank you for asking." It was not enough information for Claire but was all she could glean.

The remainder of June passed without incident and July, too. After the cool rainstorm the night of Matthew's injury, the weather warmed and stayed warm. Claire did not miss the suffocating humidity of the Indian heat. She loved the blue and green English summer and continued her morning walks faithfully, but she would catch herself looking up every once in a while as if she expected to see Symonton on Bonaparte cantering down to join her. Of course, he was hundreds of miles away from Sussex and from Claire, doing very well thank you for asking, and she was being foolish.

In late July, Walter Thatcher materialized on the Penwarrens' doorstep. Moira brought Claire his card and stepped back as if fearing an explosion. Claire stared at the calling card in horror.

"Oh, no! Is it too late to tell him I died of a fever last month?" Sophie gave a crack of laughter, but Cecelia murmured her sister's name with a gentle chiding.

"He cares for you, Claire, so don't be unkind to him."

"Please, Cece, spare me your lecture. Love has made you too charitable to live with."

"And love has made you unbearable to live with," Cecelia retorted, uncharacteristically sharp. Then she lowered her eyes to her sewing and would not let Claire draw out an explanation for the words.

Claire dragged Sophie along to the drawing room where Thatcher and the two women sat in intermittent silence. Finally Thatcher said to Claire, "Perhaps you could show me the gardens, cousin." Sophie, who had left a half-eaten tea cake on her plate, agreed with enthusiasm.

"A splendid idea! Go ahead, Claire. I'm sure your cousin will appreciate the roses," and she scurried off to finish her treat.

Once alone in the gardens, Claire tried to keep up a continuous horticultural conversation but it was one-sided at best. Finally drawing her down beside him on a bench, Thatcher repeated his proposal of marriage.

Claire disentangled her hand from his and stated firmly, "Really, Sir Walter, I do not appreciate your insistence. We had this discussion earlier in the year, and I was quite clear and definite in my answer. I cannot believe you want to expose me to discomfort again."

"That was weeks ago. I saw in the paper that your father was home, your sister was to marry, and Symonton was away for the summer. It seemed an ideal time to repeat my offer, now that all the influences that I am sure discouraged you the first time are removed." Claire stood up and tried to appear resolute with purpose.

"There were no influences that caused my refusal, Sir Walter, and I beg, I sincerely beg you not to bring up this matter again. I am very happy here, and I neither desire nor intend to marry. My father needs my company, and I would be an ungrateful daughter if I refused it. Please, let us speak no more about it."

You are a prosy fool as dense as wool, she wanted to add, and I would rather leap into a vat of boiling oil than marry you. Claire did not express herself quite that succinctly, however, so Thatcher left without giving up hope that an alliance between them might still be formed.

As much as he professed a love for the home of his childhood, it seemed to Claire that her father could seldom be found there. Visiting neighbors, he would say vaguely in response to her query about his activities, and she supposed she ought to be happy that he was fitting in to country life so comfortably. Claire could not explain it, but her father's prolonged absences, her sister's concentration on her upcoming wedding, and her brothers' spellbound attachment to Mr. Freeman's instructions all left her curiously adrift without purpose or plan. She did not like the feeling.

Claire began to spend time with the vicar, volunteering to teach a small class of renters' children to read and helping to organize the annual church fete. The latter enterprise did not go as well as the former. Claire was as used to children as she was to making all the plans and directing all the action, so she found working among a group of similarly-intentioned grown women to be trying.

"I know it may be good for me," she muttered to Sophie, "but I'm not sure my character will survive any benefit I gain from the experience."

Claire did not feel her usual cheerful and calm self, that was the problem, and when she allowed herself to probe below the surface, not being a woman to avoid difficult truth, she knew her mood had something to do with Symonton's absence. She didn't know why that should be. Except for that last chaste embrace, he had never once indicated any fondness for her stronger than that of a pet sister whose antics and words sometimes had the ability to amuse him. Yes, he had been extraordinarily kind to her on several occasions, but kindness was hardly a lover's emotion. Even if what she felt for him had anything to do with love—and having never been in love before she could not say for certain that was what it was—she could not honestly imagine that Symonton would ever look at her in that same way. Claire had no illusions about herself. She was perfectly acceptable in her appearance but no great beauty in either face or figure, she had a sharp tongue and managing ways, she would be nine and twenty in November, and while her mother had left her a comfortable consequence, it was by no means a fortune. A man like Robert, Lord Symonton, could have his pick of any young heiress or peeress he chose. He was not going to select the backwater daughter of a minor earl. Claire lectured herself sternly and continued to teach the tenants' children their letters.

In August at the breakfast table one morning, Claire's father announced, "Do you know what I think we need?"

Everyone around the table stopped in concert, utensils mid-mouth and toast half-chewed as they eyed Lord Loden seated comfortably at the head of the table. It was hard telling what their papa thought, but he was a vigorous and hearty man and they were sure it would be something unexpected.

"I think we need a party."

"A party?" Claire parroted blankly.

"Yes, a big party, Claire. You know, music and dancing and tables full of food, and we'll invite everyone in the county and celebrate well into the next morning."

"What exactly will we celebrate?" Any other time Claire would have been excited at the announcement, her head full of plans for the entertainment and the guest list and the refreshments, but that morning she was unable to generate any enthusiasm for a party, at least not one to be held in August.

Now September would be another matter all together. The thought of a party in September, in late September, made her heart sing with the prospect.

"Life, Claire," answered her father, beaming at her. "We celebrate the joys of life. Must there be a more specific reason?"

Claire, who felt she had been missing out on the joys of life for some time, protested weakly, "But we have a wedding to plan for October."

"Which is exactly why the party must be in August," her father retorted. He smiled at everyone, then pushed himself away from the table and strolled out of the breakfast room whistling a nameless melody. Claire could not decide who was acting more strangely, she or her father. It didn't matter. His heart was set on a party and so a party there would be. An August party, despite her unspoken yearning for late September

Symonton, meanwhile, had thrown himself into life at Symonton Manor with a vengeance. He had thought a separation from the intoxication of Claire Penwarren would help clear his head and perhaps cause her to miss him, if only a little bit. Remembering his conversation with William, Symonton considered this the first truly hard decision of his life where he'd had to follow through on his own advice to consider the possibilities and weigh the right and wrong of things. He was not completely sure he'd made the right decision, but he was going to stick by it and use his time at Symonton Manor profitably. He had allowed the place to fall into a casually ruinous state and was ashamed. Someday, he thought, I may bring Claire here and what will she think? What Claire thought mattered more to him than anything ever had in his entire life. He went out daily with his manager to tour his land and flocks of sheep, the tenants' homes, and the small village, also called Symonton. Everything he viewed appeared cheap and dowdy. Had his tenants always lived like this, in hovels that needed repair? Hadn't the manor itself grown dreadfully depressing since his last visit? Surely he had not spent six months out of every one of the last ten years in surroundings this drab. Yes, he'd told Claire the manor was bleak, but he had been making exaggerated conversation for effect. Now to find out it was all true, that the place was, in fact, dismal and depressing surprised and humbled him. To be scrupulously fair, however, Symonton thought it might be that anywhere Claire was not would of necessity be dreary.

He'd had his arms around her once and had been careful to take a deep breath and not do anything to startle her. He could easily have kissed her so long and so hard she'd have been dizzy and breathless. The moment he'd felt her softness pressed against him the idea of kissing her had blazoned into his mind and would not at first go away. But she had come into his arms willingly and with such trust, he'd been afraid to do anything to spoil it. Afraid to kiss Claire Penwarren—he, of all people! A man who had spent intimate time with some of the most talented—and compensated—courtesans known to the society of high-born Englishmen.

The problem was that he was out of his element with Claire and completely thrown off balance, accustomed as he was to being with women, either of good society or bad, whose sole purpose in life was to charm him into a commitment. Well-bred or not, society matrons or bits of muslin, all of them were women of practiced skills of one kind or another and expectations mutually understood. He was not used to being careful and self-controlled in either word or action because his title and fortune always guaranteed forgiveness. Now he'd fallen so low that he'd been afraid even to *kiss* a woman, devil take it! He sincerely hoped the continuation of such uncharacteristic and habitual chastity would not somehow affect his ability to take greater liberties, liberties well beyond a kiss, if he were ever able to claim Claire as his own and get her alone in a room. Their bedchamber, preferably.

"I know all this restraint may be good for me," he muttered to himself, "but I'm not sure my character will survive any benefit I gain from the experience."

Symonton received one letter from Claire, a chatty, newsy missive on engraved blush paper that did not contain a comma of sentiment, only cheerful descriptions of the gardens and amusing anecdotes about the children in her reading class. She hadn't even sprayed the note with rosewater.

Geoffrey, Symonton's valet, watched to see if the note found its way into pockets and boots again, but it didn't. Symonton put it on the desk in the library and weighted it down with a vase of wild roses. He would have Claire's fragrance with him in spite of the miles.

"We are having a party the twenty-sixth of August," she wrote toward the end of her letter. "I don't suppose you could shorten your stay in Cornwall and come in time to join us?" Claire had struggled with just the right words, keeping everything light and purposefully mentioning the festivity almost after the fact, a pastime so inconsequential she had almost forgotten about it.

As he read her letter, Symonton had a clear picture of Claire's face, thick auburn hair down and held in place by a kerchief, the sun glinting the gold flecks in her hazel eyes, her smile turned on him with all the warmth of a bonfire. Yes, he supposed he could join them on the twenty-sixth of August. Just try and keep him away.

He sent a return note equally as light. He was busy rebuilding the renters' cottages, he wrote, and was considering putting in a textile mill. The ocean was beautiful in summer. The sea spray was hard on the gardens. Oh, and by the way, he thought he might be able to make the August party and would look forward to seeing Sussex again sooner than expected.

Claire read Symonton's responding note and kept it in her pocket all day to take out whenever she had a private moment to reread. Her friend would be coming, and she suddenly found the plans for the party enthralling and exciting. Her family noted the sparkle in her eyes again but could not account for it. Not that that mattered; it was just good to have their Claire back.

Lady Pasturson and Harry joined the Penwarrens for supper one evening the week before the party. Claire had always thought her nearest neighbor an attractive woman, but that night she looked especially lovely, with soft, high color in her face and shining eyes. At the end of the meal, Lord Loden rose.

"I have an announcement to make."

Everyone around the table went suddenly quiet, their eyes fixed on Philip.

"This afternoon I spoke with Vernon, Lord Pasturson, and asked for his mother's hand in marriage. I am delighted to say that he gave it instantly so Margaret and I would not be forced to elope." A small murmur of laughter floated around the table.

"I hope those that I love best will welcome another I love into their midst."

Claire was so completely flabbergasted that for a moment she really had no idea what to say. Had everyone else known except her? She rose quickly from the table to kiss her papa on the cheek and come to Lady Margaret's side.

"How wonderful to have you as a stepmama! I couldn't be happier," and she bent to embrace the older woman as she sat.

When Claire looked up, she was conscious of a curious stillness, everyone watching her response. Had they truly been anxious about it? Did they think she would be anything but thrilled for her father, a loving and robust man who had buried three wives and borne more grief than one person should know? The odd moment of quiet was replaced by a swelling, happy buzz about the table and Claire went to the door to ask for another bottle of wine, the special French wine they had been saving for something extraordinary. It certainly suited the present occasion.

Later Cecelia came to Claire's room. "You don't mind, do you, Claire?" she asked quietly.

Claire sat deep in thought as she brushed her hair, stroking it until the strands gleamed red in the candlelight.

"Mind?" She turned to Cecelia. "I thought everyone was looking at me strangely this evening. Why ever would I mind?"

"You have been Papa's hostess for many years. You've run his household and taken care of him. Now he will have a wife to do so."

"I know, but do I seem so selfish that I would begrudge him real happiness with a loving wife as fine as Lady Margaret? I know I've made a cock-up of everything I've tried recently, but if all my family is happy, I am happy, too. Truly."

Claire meant every word she said, but she was also well aware that she must readjust her future plans. She thought it would be hard to be only a daughter in the house and decided that as soon as both weddings were over, one in October and one in December, she would return to India. There would be plenty for her to manage there, including a fine, large home, a staff of servants, and social relations in the restricted British community. There was the tea plantation, as well. Her father had the family estate in Sussex to run now and would be absent from India for long stretches of time. Perhaps he would consider teaching her the rudiments of his interests there. He had approved her eye for details and her head for figures on numerous occasions and Claire thought there must be some similarity between the particulars of domestic expertise and the successful practice of trade. With Cecelia's family there for support and company, perhaps she would not feel quite so distant from England where all her heart lived. She had been managing something or other for many years and simply couldn't imagine not *doing* something with her time and energy.

Claire planned to ask Aunt Sophie if she would be willing to take up residence in India with her because doing so seemed to make sense for both their sakes, but at breakfast the very next morning Sophie volunteered, "They've offered me the Dower House once Margaret marries. Vernon doesn't want it vacant and I'll be able to live close to my family." When she said the word *family*, her voice trembled a moment and Claire felt a quick tenderness for the older, gray-haired woman who had spent thirty unhappy years with a man of unkind and ignoble character. Claire's father did not speak of his brother willingly, only when asked, but what Claire gleaned was unpleasant and sometimes shocking. Following Sophie's pronouncement, Claire said nothing to her aunt about traveling to India. Sophie might have felt duty bound to accompany Claire and Claire would not have forced those feelings for the world. Sophie was too obviously delighted with the arrangements already made.

When Symonton came to Claire's mind, which he seemed to do more and more of late, she refused to think about him at the same time she contemplated a return to India. The certain knowledge that she would see the man only infrequently if at all once she departed British shores dimmed India's brilliant colors and made what should have been an exotic adventure seem no more than tedious. To be scrupulously fair, however, Claire thought anywhere Symonton was not would of necessity be tedious. He certainly knew how to liven up one's life.

The hall's kitchen was busy a full fortnight before the August party. Claire sat with Mrs. Feastwell and together they decided on the menu, then Feastwell went in search of several more kitchen girls from the nearby village to help.

"Get whatever you need, Mrs. Feastwell. I'm sure I trust your judgment," Claire told her. "When Papa decides to do something of this nature, do not under any circumstances skimp." So Feastwell was delightedly left to her own devices— an abundance of cream cakes and fresh fruit and even an ice sculpture! Her mind whirled with ideas.

Claire's mind whirled, as well. She had arranged for the musicians and had followed that up by sketching out how Mrs. Crayton should arrange the grounds. First choice would be the orchestra on the verandah and dancing both inside and out. They had done it that way often enough in India, where the heat often made dancing inside unbearable, and Claire thought such a dual arrangement would cause a pleasant little stir in the Sussex countryside.

The day of the party Claire was up early and dressed in her work smock, doing a final count of glasses and serving dishes, checking linens, sending the housemaids to polish silver, having chairs brought down from upstairs, handling all the last minute details at which she so excelled. The day was perfect, hot without being uncomfortable, with a clear blue sky and only the slightest of breezes, the end of August and a fitting finale to summer.

As busy as she was, Claire could not keep from straying to the closest window now and again to look for her friend. Symonton had written to say he was coming and she couldn't help but think that he might make an early appearance, just to say hello, of course, and to check on Matthew's health. So when Cecelia came to tell her she had a visitor in the front drawing room, Claire's face lit up with happy anticipation, only to feel her heart plummet so low its fall might have bruised her toes. The visitor was not—alas—Symonton.

Claire read the calling card her sister held out and cried, "This is too much, Cece! Go immediately back and tell Sir Walter that I am indisposed. No, better yet, tell him the truth, say I cannot see him because if I do, I will murder him and I do not wish his blood on my hands, not on this particular afternoon, at least, though I daresay any other afternoon it would not bother me at all."

Moira, standing just outside the door, congratulated herself for having the good sense to ask Miss Cecelia to deliver the gentleman's card. She could picture Miss Claire doing something violent or at least inelegant, and a murder, which could rightfully be said to fit into both categories, would not surprise her at all.

"Claire, just see him for a moment. He is your cousin, after all."

"He is an idiot," Claire fumed, "and as dull-witted as a herring. Do I look like I have time to meet with a man whose inability to understand English is surpassed only by his inability to maintain rational thought?" At Cecelia's mute look—she was perceptive enough to know that her sister's question was purely rhetorical—Claire stamped her foot and repeated crossly, "This really is too much, you know." Then she met her sister's look and both women suddenly began to laugh, helplessly, choking on giggles, wiping away tears that ran down their cheeks, and clutching onto each other for support.

"Oh, Cece, I think I really may have to murder the man," but Claire smiled when she spoke.

She purposefully did not change but went to meet Mr. Thatcher dressed as she was, tendrils of hair coming loose and dirt smudges along her hem. Her cousin frowned a little, making it a point to note her dishevelment and then quickly look away to pretend it didn't matter.

"How very lovely you look, cousin! So rustic in your country dress." Claire really did want to thump him.

"You've caught me at a very bad time, Sir Walter, because we are hosting a festivity at the hall this evening."

"But I've come all the way from London just to see you," he said, certain that anything—even a community-wide festivity celebrating the engagement of the head of the family—that interfered with his plans should be rescheduled to allow him to accomplish his purpose.

There was a long pause through which Claire clenched her jaw and gritted her teeth. She was not, absolutely and irrevocably not, going to invite her cousin to the evening's party and have him following her around making offensive chatter and asking her to dance every time she turned a corner.

But even as she made that mental resolution, Claire said aloud, "Are you staying locally, Sir Walter?" When he mentioned the nearby inn, she responded as graciously as she could. "Then you must by all means consider yourself invited this evening." Thatcher caught her hand in his and she immediately attempted to pull it free as he spoke.

"How very, very kind of you, my dear cousin. I knew if I gave you enough time you would see me in a more compatible light. You were just too isolated in that heathen country to be perfectly comfortable with our civilized society and no doubt frightened and —dare I say it?— awe-struck by my importunate offers. Of course, that is only to be expected from one so delicately bred. You needed to become more at ease in your mind with my companionship. I can only say that I have grown very fond of your good sense and tractability and would be honored if you would accept my suit."

"No, no, no, no, no!" cried Claire, rapidly losing her good humor and once again having to wrest her hand free from Thatcher's grasp. "Really, this is too unkind of you, Sir Walter, when I particularly asked you not to bring this matter up in my presence again. I am not delicately bred and I am not in the least tractable. Not. In. The. Least. I assure you we would not suit at all."

From the doorway Symonton drawled, "She is absolutely right, Thatcher. I know for a fact that Lady Claire is not possessed of the tiniest bit of tractability." He was laughing and meeting her gaze with such directness that Thatcher might not have been in the room at all. Claire felt that someone had suddenly pulled back the draperies from all the windows and let in streams of blinding sunshine.

Symonton came forward, stepping adroitly between Thatcher and Claire, and took both of Claire's hands in his.

"I came as soon as I received your message. I can't tell you how distressed I was. Don't tell me it's the plumbing again." Symonton loved watching the expression on Claire's face when she had to scramble like this.

"No, your lordship, fortunately it is not the plumbing this time. Your expert advice was so invaluable in London—and really, who would have imagined you knew so very much about plumbing?—that I am sure we will not see a repeat of *that* problem. No, it's, it's—" Symonton waited with a smiling lack of assistance. "—it's Babu!" Claire returned Symonton's look with a triumphant one of her own.

"Babu? Oh, my. What exactly is the problem and how may I help?"

"The poor thing chased some unknown creature up a tree, quite, quite far up a tree, up into the highest branches, and now he's stuck there. Yes, stuck there, unable or unwilling—Babu being nearly as intractable as I—to come down. The whole family is worried to distraction, so, my lord, I immediately thought of you, recalling the affectionate regard you have long held for Babu, and how he dotes on your every tone. I thought—"

"That I might climb the tree, Lady Claire, to rescue him? At the risk of appearing heartless regarding Babu's unfortunate predicament, I am hardly dressed for tree climbing."

Claire had to agree. His lordship wore a deep blue coat and crisp white shirt, a perfectly folded cravat and blue doeskin trousers that fit him so closely and so well she wondered why she had been surprised to hear that he was a proficient fighter. How could she have missed all that muscle? Too busy enjoying those sky blue eyes, she thought, eyes that showed especially piercing at the moment against a face that had browned over the summer and hair that had gone a shade whiter. Claire could not recall ever being so happy to see anyone in her life.

"Of course, I wouldn't expect you to climb the tree, your lordship. However, I thought —I hoped — you might be willing to crouch at the base of the tree and call his name in an inviting manner." The picture of the elegant gentleman in front of her doing exactly that so tickled Claire that she laughed out loud, at the last minute turning the giggle into a small fit of coughing.

Symonton proffered a crisp, white handkerchief. "Not coming down with an illness, I trust."

Thatcher, who had been standing speechless during the entire verbal exchange, asked plaintively, "But who is Babu?"

To which question Symonton answered calmly, "What luck, Thatcher! You are able to meet Babu for yourself because here he is."

With the excruciating contrariness of feline timing, the white cat strolled into the drawing room, jumped onto a small loveseat by the door, and began to give his right hind leg a vigorous and thorough bath.

"Well," said Claire in a voice curiously devoid of emotion, "how extraordinary! He was up a tree just a moment ago."

"Extraordinary indeed," agreed Symonton, "considering how *quite, quite far up* the tree you said he was. They say cats have nine lives and apparently Babu continues to work his way through all of his."

"Cats are very perceptive and their senses are highly developed," contributed Claire soberly. "My belief is that based on his extravagant regard for you, Babu discerned that you were in the general vicinity and the happy realization was all he needed to find the fortitude to descend the tree."

"Surely not an *extravagant* regard, Lady Claire. Such esteem from so discriminating a feline does me too great an honor. I am wholly undeserving."

By then the entire conversation had grown too inexplicable for Thatcher, who gave Symonton a sour look, reached for Claire's hand, barely missed it as she thrust it behind her back, and said, "I will look forward to this evening, cousin. I only hope my city dress won't outshine your country neighbors to any of their discomfort. I did not bring anything appropriate for rusticating with the natives."

Claire, who could not trust herself to speak, made a little motion with her hand toward the door. It was Symonton that took the other man's arm and escorted him out of the room. When he returned, he saw that Claire had tried to do something with her hair—unsuccessfully since little curls still fell loose around her face. He thought she looked enchanting.

"Has he been making your life miserable?" he asked with sympathy, his tone so companionable they might not have been separated for weeks.

"You can't know. He continues to work under the delusion that I secretly wish to marry him but am too shy and retiring and apparently mentally confused to tell him so. But never mind him, Symonton, when did you get back?"

"Yesterday afternoon late."

"So you know about your sister and Papa."

"Margaret wrote about it first, and she and I discussed it last evening."

"Is it all right with you? I know Papa cares for her very much and she seems to have lost twenty years over the summer." Symonton had thought so, too. His sister had loved her first husband and deeply grieved his passing, but he thought the depth of happiness she wore now had not been there at her first marriage.

"My sister is of age, Claire, so even if I didn't approve, which is not the case, she could still do whatever she chose."

"But you know she would not want to displease you. She's awfully fond of you, Symon."

As I wish you were, he thought, but answered, "I know, and I am certainly not displeased. Nevertheless, other than a brief introduction the day of his arrival, I have yet to meet your father properly. Is he nearby that I may do so? And how is young Matt?"

"All recovered. His arm healed straight and strong and Mr. Freeman is teaching him all the unpleasant cant of fighting: facers and—and—well, I don't know any other words, but you understand what I mean. Now let me go and get Papa, since I know he will want to see you."

She was chattering happily and he was somewhere between listening to and watching her. Claire's face was so transparent, he would know her mood even if he couldn't hear a word she spoke.

When Symonton stood before her father, he again noted the resemblance: the same clear brow, hazel eyes, and genuine smile as Claire. No wonder his sister had lost her heart. Robert, Lord Loden, was a handsome man with an expressive face and easy manners.

"Claire, Lord Symonton and I will spend some time in the library," Loden said. "Didn't I hear that Feastwell needed you?" Claire gave a little gasp.

"The petit fours!" she exclaimed without explanation and standing on tiptoe kissed her father on the cheek. To Symonton she said, "How lovely to have you home, Symon! I'll see you tonight," and was gone, the scent of rosewater trailing behind her.

Symonton, his gaze following her out of the room despite his best attempt at indifference, turned back to find Claire's father eyeing him with wisdom and the same warm, practical humor that was often on Claire's face.

"So it's like that, is it?" the older man asked.

"Yes," said Symonton, "it's exactly like that."

At that moment the two men decided they liked each other very much and strolled off together to discuss the women in their lives.

Chapter 10

*E*verything was going splendidly, Claire thought. Sounds of laughter and music filled the night air, refreshments were delicious and plentiful and the house and the grounds beautiful. It was the perfect night she had hoped for, besides, the sky crowded with stars all smiled upon by a large white moon.

Cecelia looked radiant in emerald green silk with her hand resting proprietarily on Harry's arm, and Papa and Lady Pasturson—Claire must decide what exactly to call her stepmother after the wedding—were so obviously happy it made her smile just to see them together. The lovely evening made all the frantic planning and rushing about worthwhile.

From the corner where she stood, she saw Symonton enter and scan the room, looking for someone, looking for her apparently, for when his glance reached her, he smiled and crossed the room immediately to her side. He had never done that before, had always seemed to meander in her direction as if she were an afterthought, and Claire felt flattered and pleased by the attention.

"You look lovely," he said. His love wore a gown of creamy white satin embroidered with white flowers traced in gold thread and over the satin a diaphanous skirt stitched with more gold and silver. All the gold thread reflected the lights and somehow showed again in her eyes. Her shoulders were bare, and it was hard to tell exactly where the creamy white satin of the dress stopped and her skin began. Her hair, parted down the middle and arranged in a coiled plait at the back of her neck, was the color of sunlit autumn leaves. Everything about her showed soft and lovely. If he ever took Claire to Symonton Manor, he thought she would make that drab place shine the moment she crossed the threshold. After talking with her father that afternoon, Symonton hoped there might be a chance for that very thing to happen.

Claire looked down at her dress and gave a little grimace.

"Thank you, but at the risk of sounding like my cousin Walter, I worry the gown is a little too grand for a country evening, but it was too late to change my mind or my gown. I feel like Titania in *A Midsummer Night's Dream*."

"'Why art thou here, come from the farthest steppe of India?'" quoted Symonton with a smile, then added, "Forgive me if I offend but speaking of Titania brings Bottom to mind, and from there it is a natural progression to your cousin Walter. Is he present this evening?"

Symonton had no sooner asked the question and Claire responded with a little chuckle than they both saw Thatcher making his way purposefully toward them. With a serendipitous air, the musical quartet started up at the same time and Symonton pulled Claire out the door to the side porch and then to the adjoining dance floor she'd had constructed on the lawn.

"This is a charming idea, Claire," his lordship said, looking about him. "Was it yours?"

"We did it often in India to cope with the heat. There's something quite magical about dancing under the stars."

Symonton, holding Claire as the melodic country dance began, had to agree, but he thought the presence of stars had little to do with what he felt. He'd have found it magical even if it began to snow.

Claire had to leave after the one dance, but they came together periodically throughout the evening for a quick word or smile. He felt disappointed that he did not have another chance to hold her, but Claire had hostess duties and was forced to stay one step ahead of Thatcher besides.

Oddly enough, despite her constant activity there was never a moment during the whole evening when Claire did not know exactly where Symonton was. With an almost mystical prescience, she was aware of his presence even as she greeted guests, made introductions, complimented the young women, and conferred with Crayton. Of course, Symonton was hard to miss with his gleaming hair turned to white gold from constant summer excursions across his vast Cornwall estate and that cavalier look about him that left admiring glances and raised eyebrows in his wake. He really was offensively cool sometimes, and she caught the Ice Man expression on his face more than once, indicating that someone either bored him or had grown too familiar. Twice she considered going to his rescue but thought better of it both times. He was an adult, after all, and she was not his keeper, only his friend. Toward the end of the evening, Symonton made his way once more to Claire.

"The evening is a great success, Claire. I congratulate you."

"It is a success, isn't it?" she replied with satisfaction, looking around her and thinking wistfully how much she would miss the role of hostess when her father married. "I did so want it to be exactly right for Papa and Lady Margaret. They will live here with the boys."

"And with you, as well."

"I doubt that would do, Symonton," Claire admitted frankly. "I told you once that I was spoiled and used to making decisions, so I think having to be the spinster daughter of the house, living on the coattails of my family would make me and everyone around me miserable. Your sister deserves better than having to tiptoe about for fear she will hurt my feelings if she wants to change the color of the morning room. She's very kind and I am afraid she would feel obligated to include me in domestic decisions, an arrangement that would eventually prove awkward and unpleasant for both of us. Loden Hall is her home now, not mine. No, I will go back to India as soon as the weddings are past. Our old home is there and can use a managing female. I will not stay year round, of course, not with all my family here, but there is enough in India to keep me busy six months out of every year, at least, and you know I am happiest when I stay busy."

Startled to hear her plans, Symonton tried to formulate a reply that would not expose the panic he felt at the idea of her departure, but the musicians gave a quick, tuneful flourish and her father stepped up on the dais where the musicians sat. It was clear he wished to make a speech. Claire, seeing his broad smile and beaming face, could not recall her father ever looking happier.

"My family and I are pleased to have so many friends and neighbors with us this evening. It has been a year of change for my children and for me, and while I regret the sad demise of my brother, I cannot regret the happiness that our coming to the Loden Valley has brought to my daughter Cecelia and to me. I am delighted to announce my engagement to the most beautiful and charming woman in the world." He reached out and brought

Margaret to his side, her hand in his and her eyes in the lamplight shining—perhaps with tears, it was difficult to tell. A ripple of conversation started and swelled, followed by a sincere round of applause. Lady Pasturson had lived there many years and was well loved.

"Of course, we also share the happy news of my daughter Cecelia's engagement to Harry Macapee." That was already public knowledge, but there was another round of kind applause, nevertheless. "When Cecelia first met Harry, he planned a military career and my daughter was content with the prospect, but once I met my future son-in-law I decided I was not about to share him with the army."

At those words, Claire looked at her father more sharply. What he was about to announce would be as much a surprise to her as to all the other listeners.

"I know his mother will shed some tears, but after their marriage, Harry and Cecelia will return to India to run our home there and learn the tea business. I cannot think of anyone I would trust more with the undertaking, and I have every confidence that Harry will be a success, especially since my Cecelia comes from an honorable and influential family of the region who will no doubt be eager to support her and her new husband."

Symonton watched a range of emotions pass across Claire's face, shock at first, followed by a quick disappointment that shadowed despair, and then only resolute happiness. She went immediately to her sister and whispered something to her, at which Cecelia stepped back and searched Claire's face intently, her own dark eyes fixed on her sister. Then evidently finding whatever it was she sought, Cecelia smiled and put her arms around her sister in a hug, whispering something to Claire in return. The little tableau lasted only a moment before Claire turned away, smiling, to make a remark to Harry. Unless one knew her well, Symonton thought, unless one loved her, she would have appeared the same as an hour ago, happy at the occasion, delighted with the news, and proud of her home and family. He did know her well, however, loved her, too, and he realized that something had changed for his Claire in some private place she would not allow anyone to see.

Symonton was almost right, but not exactly. Claire had indeed been stunned and for a moment despairing. All this time she had foreseen herself doing what Harry would be doing, going where Cecelia would be going. She had already begun to plan time with their Indian estate manager to better understand the climate and conditions for tea. She had visions of making changes in the house, too, new colors in the downstairs rooms and a wider verandah, a small gazebo for the yard and more wild roses in the garden. She had even thought that Cecelia could come and stay with her when Harry was away. Claire could not picture the reverse, however. It would not work that she should go and live with Harry and Cecelia. Poor Cece would feel forced to ask Claire's opinion at every turn, and Claire herself, although she loved her sister dearly, knew that her years of being in charge would not die a natural death. She could see herself countermanding Cece's orders out of habit and without conscious thought. It simply would not do, any more than being the dutiful spinster daughter in her father's home would do. Being the one directed was not in her nature. She had been the one doing the directing for too many years, and through no one's fault she could not change.

Claire may have despaired at first hearing her father's intentions, but the feeling did not last long. Through the years, all she had ever wanted, sincerely and with the truest affection, was her family's happiness. How could she lose heart when her father wore a constantly joyful and content expression and her sister need not be separated from her husband? Her brothers would have the steadying influence of their father and not just the fretting of an older sister. Aunt Sophie would have a home exactly the right size and in a place where she felt comfortable and appreciated. She, Claire, could not find it anywhere in her heart to be resentful or upset that it was her plans that had been disrupted. There must be other options for her future, and she lay awake long after the party was over, into the early morning hours, considering alternatives.

Despite the short night, Claire was up the next morning early enough to attend Sunday matins and still be home before anyone else in the household had risen. She had left the constructed dance floor in place and invited all the household help, the local villagers, and the laborers and tenants from the countryside to use Sunday afternoon for a gathering of their own. Even the vicar, disinclined to approve of dancing on the Lord's Day, said he thought the idea would be a pleasant pastime for his hard-working parish. Moira volunteered two fiddlers she knew of who lived nearby to be impromptu musicians for the occasion. Claire told Mrs. Crayton to set out the leftover food on tables in the yard and let people enjoy what was practically the last day of summer. It was still August, but too soon the tang of fall would be here and then the cold, dead days of winter.

"Everyone should have a party," Claire had declared to Crayton. "I'm sure they will appreciate the chance to bid summer farewell." With an inward smile, Claire thought if she was no longer needed to manage her family, she would manage her neighbors instead.

She spent Sunday afternoon sitting lazily on the western porch, enjoying the music and laughter that came from the yard below, thinking a little sadly that she would miss Sussex and Loden Hall but feeling no despair or worry at all. She had formed a plan that made comfortable sense and her mind was at ease. How fortunate she was, Claire thought with gratitude, not to be a woman to mope or brood for very long!

Symonton rode out on Bonaparte both Monday and Tuesday mornings, planning a falsely fortuitous meeting with Claire, hoping to see her striding along, walking stick in one hand and her hair caught up under a straw hat with just enough curls showing to tease. She did not appear either morning. When she finally did materialize early Wednesday, Symonton suddenly and completely forgot how impatient he'd been at her absence. Just seeing her dear figure striding in the distance made the wait worthwhile.

Claire looked up when she heard Bonaparte and this time Symonton didn't think he imagined the welcoming happiness he saw on her face at his approach. She had a smile for everyone—except possibly her cousin Walter—but surely the light on her face when she saw him was more than the reflection of the morning sun.

"I was just thinking of you," Claire declared without guile, "and wondering if you were up yet. I knew you'd say goodbye before you left for London or returned to Cornwall. Will you stay through both the weddings now?"

Claire's father and Lady Pasturson had at first planned to wait until after Harry and Cecelia's nuptials, but with the impatience of much younger lovers they had decided to move their wedding day from December to late September. It would be a quieter, less public ceremony than their children's wedding and much easier to prepare for. On a practical note, their being wed would give them greater freedom to host receptions and welcome houseguests for the October marriage of the younger couple.

"Yes, but at the moment I feel completely out of place in my sister's household. The topics of dresses and flowers are so foreign to me that I am regularly driven to the stables to clear my head." Claire smiled sympathy without slowing her brisk pace.

"I can't imagine that, Symonton. Surely you have had some kind of education in those subjects with at least one of your lady friends."

"Yes, but it was not the same thing at all."

"No?"

"It was never *marriage* dresses and flowers, Claire. Quite the contrary." She laughed out loud.

"That may be, Symonton, but naïve country lass that I am, when I use the term lady friends, I mean it in a literal and unremarkably proper sense."

"I've noted that you are often tediously literal," Symonton responded and Claire laughed again. She was happy to be with him but not willing to define the reasons for the pleasure his companionship gave her. What could it matter? He was her friend and that must be enough; she would enjoy his company while she could. She knew he had been separated from London society for several months and must undoubtedly desire to return to a place that offered pastimes to fit his active life. That he had rusticated in the wilds of the Cornwall wilderness all those weeks and then returned to the bucolic countryside instead of haring straight off to fleshpots still surprised her.

Even more, she thought he might feel as displaced by his sister's marriage as she by her father's, the close bond of brother and sister replaced by Margaret's relationship with her new husband. Claire felt a sympathetic kinship with Symonton on that level and understood why he might wish to leave Sussex as soon as possible. She felt much the same. Running from, not to.

They reached their favorite spot, the little arrangement of rocks that doubled as a sitting room, and Symonton took a seat where he could see his darling's face clearly without glare or shadow.

"What will you do now, Claire?"

She did not pretend to misunderstand him but took off the soft, worn garden hat she had grabbed that morning from the kitchen and casually ran a hand through her hair before answering.

"I admit I was momentarily addled when I first heard Papa's plans, but they make perfect sense. I'm relieved that Cece will not be alone months out of every year or need to follow her husband around the globe to places that might be at best uncomfortable and at worst dangerous. I hope I am not so self-absorbed that I think everyone must arrange their lives to suit me. It's all for the best. Just think what you've saved, Symonton, by not having to buy your nephew a commission. I daresay you can find better things to do with that money."

"Yes," he said, looking at her and thinking how magnificent she would look in silk the color of Indian rubies, "I can."

"I also confess that it took me a while to get past the idea that I was doomed to be a family hanger-on. The thought of drifting from family member to family member, the bane of my brothers' wives and always the extra person at table, made me shudder. I know I could not bear that. It's not the same for me as it is for you, Symonton. I can't enter university or learn a trade to support myself. Perhaps that will be an avenue for women someday, but neither is an option for my present-day dilemma. I must live within the constraints society allows and do so in a way that will not discomfit my family." Claire's voice dropped off.

Considering what might have been but will never be, Symonton thought with a lover's clarity, and felt a great tenderness for her.

She was brisk again. "But now, I've thought of a way to balance my desire for a level of independence against the strictures of the world in which I live. I'd had my original plans set for such a while that it was hard to divest myself of them and start anew, but I am nothing if not adaptable." She looked over at him with a triumphant air. "Once I put my mind to it, I hardly needed any time at all to come up with an alternate plan. I know exactly what I will do once the weddings and the holiday are past."

"I find," he drawled, enjoying her more than he could possibly say, "that I am aflutter with expectation. What exactly are these plans with which you are so self-satisfied?"

"Don't mock me, Symonton. It isn't becoming in you and you should know by now it does not intimidate me. Did I ever mention that I have an inheritance from my mother?"

"I believe you once said something about it in passing."

"Of course, it's not so very much—not a Symonton type of inheritance, I mean," she grinned over at him, "but I have been calculating for nearly two days now and I believe it is enough to keep me in a modest home with some small pin money for many years. I will need to be thrifty and cannot take up residence in London with its exorbitant rents, and I'm sure it will not be a very luxurious house, not like our house on Millefore, which would be too grand and too large for my tastes. But as you know I didn't enjoy London very much, and I can assure you that is not sour grapes on my part. I believe Bath will suit." She peeked over at her companion to see how he reacted to her choice of locations but could not read anything on that inscrutable face. He watched her with a steady, slightly amused regard.

"I have heard Bath is quite reasonable," Claire added, conscious by then that she was talking too much but feeling an inexplicable desire to explain herself further. "The vicar's wife told me there are tasteful small houses to let quite inexpensively in Bath. I will not have a lot of expenses, you know. Moira will come with me and I hope Babu but that's all, and I can live very modestly. It's not as if I am just out of the schoolroom, so I cannot think anyone will find it objectionable that I live alone. Besides, I can always invite Aunt Sophie for a visit to lend me countenance and scotch any unpleasant talk. I'm not really used to solitary living, but I have family to visit if I grow lonely and to celebrate special occasions." Claire faltered for a moment, picturing a house empty of the noise of family, no boys shouting down the hallway, no Cece practicing on the piano forte. She wondered how long it would take for her to grow accustomed to such a solitary life.

"I know there won't be many people for me to order around and you well understand what pleasure I find in doing so, but I am determined to be less interfering and more pliable and conciliatory. I would not want my managing ways to make me intolerable to my family as their own families grow. Your sister is the kindest of women but I think even she would box my ears if I dared to command her kitchen." Claire stopped her flow of chatter and concluded with a rueful twist to her mouth that made him want to kiss away the expression. "You may not believe this but I have learned some valuable lessons this year. I now realize that I do not always know best." At his continued silence, she stirred slightly and asked, "Well, what do you think, Symon?"

"I think you are the most adorable idiot I have ever met in all my advanced years." It was not the response she had expected and neither was the expression in his eyes, a laughing look full of tenderness and another emotion that caused her heart to begin beating abnormally fast. "You are not going to do anything of the sort, my darling, no house in Bath, no old maid cap, no spinster aunt visits to your family. I am willing to tolerate devil cat but the rest is the height of absurdity, and if I didn't love you so desperately and so completely, I would be laughing out loud at your outlandish plan. Although for all I care, you may go to university *and* learn a trade if that's what it takes to make you happy. Making you happy, Claire, is my one goal in life."

"What did you say?" All the color had drained from her face as she listened to his words, and she could only stare at Symonton as he sat there speaking as casually about loving her as if he were commenting on the weather.

"I said you could go to univer—"

"No, no, that other part," she interrupted peevishly.

"You mean the part where I said I love you, love you more than life, love everything about you and have loved you for months? That part?"

Claire stared at him with such mute and baffled astonishment that it was all he could do to keep from leaping to his feet and pulling her forcefully into his arms. The woman needed to be kissed, confound it all. Kissed relentlessly and passionately. Needed to find out that he was perfectly able and more than willing to introduce her to the delights of proximity. Very real delights. Very close proximity. Not quite time yet, however, he judged. Almost, but not quite. Restrain yourself, Symonton, he told himself firmly, or you risk losing the prize when you are almost at the moment of victory. So instead of following his desire for the carnal—and how often had he ever chosen to exercise that kind of restraint?—he held up one hand and shook his head at her in mock reproval.

"I can see that in your painfully literal way you wish to point out that that is not *exactly* what I said the first time, so let me think. I believe I said—" He paused for effect and had the satisfaction of seeing that beautiful breast inhale and literally stop breathing as she strained to hear him. "—that if I didn't love you so desperately and so completely, I would be laughing out loud. Yes, that's how I phrased it."

Claire exhaled at the words. Being no fool, she had always recognized that Symonton was fond of her, even that he enjoyed her company. Sometimes, particularly when she said or did something to make him laugh with a spontaneity at odds with the air of ennui he cultivated, she had even spied a flash of warmth in his glance, a warmth with the ability to pick up the beat of her heart. But until the recent betrothal celebration he had never sought her out at social gatherings with specific intent, never looked for her upon his arrival at any assembly, never danced more than once with her, never was in the least familiar in any way, never lover like at all. So she attributed the warmth to friendship and convinced herself it was enough. But now with his words dancing in the clear morning air between them, Claire realized friendship with the man in front of her, a man that bore no resemblance to the cool, jaded Symonton whom she had first met months ago, would never be enough. There had been no sparkle in *that* man's eyes, no fire, no promise of delight, no impudent grin. No love. Everything that she saw displayed in front of her at that moment.

"But you can't love me, Symon, not me." Her words came out small and breathless in nothing like her usual firm voice. She felt she had swallowed a butterfly that was trying desperately to get out of her body, its wings beating in her stomach and then pressing against her lungs and finally fluttering up into her throat so that she couldn't speak properly.

At the confused meekness in her tone—he never liked to hear his Claire humble—he stood and took two wide steps to stand in front of her. Reaching down, he took her hands in both of his and drew her to her feet.

"Yes," he said, "I can. I do," and pulled Claire into his arms and kissed her. Relentlessly, passionately, and with such ardor that they both risked collapsing from lack of air. He was gratified that she did not recoil, that instead, after just a moment, he felt two arms creep up around his neck and pull his head down even closer to her own. She made a small sound, some murmur of pleasure under his mouth, which confirmed for him that the passion he had glimpsed in her was there to be fanned into flame. What a delightful prospect for both of them!

After a while, silently holding Claire and inhaling the rosewater fragrance of her hair, Symonton felt her breathing begin to slow. The thought that she trusted him so completely that she would relax against him without self-consciousness made him feel—what? Protective? Amorous? Humble? He was familiar with only one of the three emotions and surprised they could all exist simultaneously in a man. He supposed life with Claire would expose him to all sorts of new discoveries. Symonton started to speak, heard his raspy tone, cleared his throat, and tried again.

"You are the one that advised me to marry, after all, Claire, and from the start I knew better than to resist such a deliciously managing female."

"When did I ever give you such impertinent advice?" She pulled back to look up at him, high color in her cheeks, her lips distractingly red, almost bruised in color, and her hair disheveled, the picture of a woman who has recently been ruthlessly kissed.

"I remember distinctly that you told me I needed a wife to refurbish Symonton Manor and with a summer to think about it, I decided you were right."

Claire was relieved to find her senses returning and tried to regain something of their former casual banter. For a few minutes her body had seemed to have a mind all its own, if that made any sense, and she had acted in ways that had come quite instinctively but also as a complete surprise to her. How and when had she learned to kiss with such abandon? Claire supposed she had a great deal to learn about pleasing a husband and decided from the way she had felt at Symon's handling of her that she would enjoy every moment of her education.

"It's not very often that you think I'm right or do what I suggest," Claire pointed out, forcing her mind away from such prurient thoughts. She would regain their typical easy banter at all costs, even if every part of her except one bothersome small whisper of good sense would rather be banter-free and right back in the man's arms.

Symonton was calming, too, and realized how desperately Claire was attempting to restore their conduct to something resembling normalcy. He enjoyed the self-conscious color in her cheeks but still decided to assist her in the attempt. He would not tell her that any person of maturity or experience would immediately identify the reason for the current rosy, wanton color of her face. The two of them must, sadly, make their way back to Loden Hall, and he did not want her embarrassed any more than was necessary.

"When haven't I followed your orders to the letter? Every time you told me to be quiet and go away, I did exactly what you asked."

"Symon—"

"Robert, please."

For a moment the idea of calling him by his Christian name seemed as intimate as the wedding night, but his tone had been untypically shy when he made the request and she appreciated that in his own way he had asked something of her that meant a great deal to him. Something as simple as a name.

"Robert, you are being ridiculous. I have never told you to be quiet *or* to go away."

"Your memory is conveniently selective, Claire. Will I have to accustom myself to that practice after we are wed? Well, I suppose there are worse characteristics. I can vividly recall that on more than one occasion you told me to do both those things and without a please or thank you, mind you. To my credit and like the sheep I have become, I dutifully departed each time exactly as directed and without complaint."

The little vertical line began to crease her brow as she considered his words and he quickly kissed her again. At the moment he did not want her lost in thought about anything except him, and he decided the moment was right for the words he had been rehearsing for days.

"Do you think you could learn to love me, Claire, even a little bit, and will you marry me? Before you answer either of those questions, you should know that I absolutely cannot live without you. If you say no, I will be forced to throw myself off the Bristol pier in despair." For all the teasing tone, Claire watched the smile in his eyes warm into some flaring, deep emotion that threatened to engulf her. How had she ever thought his blue eyes cold when what was in them at that moment had the potential to set her on fire?

"I would never want to be responsible for such a tragedy," she told him, then added quietly, "I would very much like to marry you, Robert. I must have loved you for quite some time because ever since we were together in London, I was never able to be completely happy unless you were near, and when you left for Cornwall— Well, my unfortunate family bore the brunt of my misery all summer until your appearance magically made everything right again."

"According to you, I have that same effect on Babu." Claire laughed and reached to pull Symonton's head down close enough for her lips to hover against his.

"Oh, no, my love," she whispered, her breath against his skin making him shiver with an emotion he thought he had lost years ago, along with his youth, along with his innocence, "not the same effect at all." After a moment of teasing proximity, she kissed him with an expertise that made Symonton think with astonishment, before he lost the ability for rational thought all together, that the future promised to hold a lifetime of such intemperate conjugal surprises.

Much, much later, the two walked hand in hand toward Loden Hall with Bonaparte trailing along behind. There was not much talking by then, just the ridiculously blissful feeling that comes with knowing one is loved, an expectation both had abandoned years ago and which consequently had an even more powerful effect on their feelings. *Dreamy* would not have been an inaccurate description of their shared mood.

So when Claire stopped abruptly it took Symonton a moment to realize that she stood before him, hands on her hips, looking as if she had just been struck by the most incredible thought she had ever experienced.

"Robert," she asked, her voice a peculiar combination of hope and anxiety, "do you think—?"

"What?" he demanded with no hint of drawl or laziness in his voice. "Do I think we will be happy? Do I think I will make a suitable husband for you and will I love you even more as the years pass? As much as the power lies in me, my darling, the answer is yes. Yes and yes and yes."

Without speaking, she turned and went into his arms a moment, expressed her approval of his passionate declaration, then took his hand and began to walk again.

"Very pretty, Robert, but what I was going to say was, do you think our engagement will finally be enough to convince cousin Walter that I will not marry him?"

"You may leave cousin Walter to me, dear heart."

"But you don't know how thick he is, Robert, really. I warn you."

Symonton looked over at Claire with her eyes alight in the sun, that astonishing mouth smiling just at him, and all her glorious hair shoved back up under her hat as if he had not just spent the last hour running his hands through her curls.

"Your cousin and I will need only one small discussion and the matter will be resolved. You may trust me on this, Claire. I will not have him distress you any longer, and I have no intention of sharing you with anyone."

"Of course, you don't," Claire agreed soothingly, "and while that thought certainly never crossed my mind, I can see that it might weigh heavily on yours, considering your earlier unfortunate experience of the heart with Cordelia."

"You have the wrong drama, Claire. It was Hamlet's Ophelia, not Lear's Cordelia."

"Oh, that's right. Ophelia. Forgive me, I always confuse the tragedies. I can only assure you, Robert, that I do not have a husband living over the stables or a husband living anywhere, for that matter. I don't pretend to know a great deal about husbands but from our recent interactions—" she had paused to find the proper word to describe the morning's mutual activities and by her expression was dissatisfied with her choice—"I sincerely believe that one husband will be quite enough for me."

Symonton turned toward Claire, tried to look stern but failed miserably, and put both arms around her waist.

"I can absolutely guarantee that," he said and kissed her so thoroughly that she eventually pulled away, breathless and flustered.

"I cannot imagine why anyone would call you Ice Man."

"I forbid you to use that name." Symonton thought he might have to kiss her once more just to prove how serious he was on that particular point. Claire smiled meekly.

"Whatever you say, Robert." There was a little pause as she once more righted her hat. "I must remind you, however, that as you once so astutely observed, I am not possessed of the tiniest bit of tractability."

And to prove how truly undutiful she was, through all the years of their happy marriage, through children and grandchildren and nieces and nephews running in and out of the bright, jewel-toned rooms of Symonton Manor, through countless clowders of white kittens with a preference for mutton, through love and laughter and some few tears, Claire boldly and defiantly continued to call her husband "Ice Man." She did not wholly lack in deference, however, for she always did so in a whisper and only during those private moments when it was very apparent to them both that he was nothing of the sort.

Claire, After All

If you enjoyed *Claire, After All*, don't stop here. Reacquaint yourself with the Penwarrens and especially with the younger of the twins, William Penwarren — all grown up, scientist and explorer extraordinaire. Despite traversing the globe, Will finds out that none of his rare discoveries of flora and fauna can hold a candle to Abby Waterston, who saves his life and steals his heart all at the same time. Read the whole story in *Listening to Abby*.

Books by Karen J. Hasley

The Penwarrens
Claire, After All * *Listening to Abby* * *Jubilee Rose*

The Laramie Series
Lily's Sister * *Waiting for Hope* * *Where Home Is*
Circled Heart * *Gold Mountain* * *Smiling at Heaven*

and *The Dangerous Thaw of Etta Capstone*

CPSIA information can be obtained at www.ICGtesting.com
Printed in the USA
LVOW10s1921141015

458267LV00001B/18/P

9 781500 665265